SWEET ILLUSIONS

SWEET ILLUSIONS

Walter Dean Myers

Teachers & Writers Collaborative

5 Union Square West, New York, N.Y. 10003

Sweet Illusions

Funding for this publication has been provided by the New York City Youth Bureau, the New York State Council on the Arts, and the National Endowment for the Arts.

Teachers & Writers Collaborative programs and publications are also made possible by funding from American Broadcasting Companies, Inc., American Can Company Foundation, American Stock Exchange, Columbia Committee for Community Service, Consolidated Edison Company, General Electric Foundation, Herman Goldman Foundation, KIDS Fund, Long Island Community Foundation, Mobil Foundation, Inc., Morgan Guaranty Trust Company, Morgan Stanley Foundation, New York Foundation for the Arts' Artist-in-Residence Program (supported by funds from the National Endowment for the Arts), New York Telephone, The New York Times Company Foundation, Henry Nias Foundation, Overseas Shipholding Group, Inc., Pisces Foundation, Helena Rubinstein Foundation, and The Scherman Foundation.

This book is dedicated to June and Chester Hopson, friends.

Teachers & Writers Collaborative
5 Union Square West
New York, N.Y. 10003

Library of Congress Cataloging-in-Publication Data

Myers, Walter Dean, 1937–
    Sweet illusions.

    Summary: A story about teenage pregnancy involving Harry, Jennifer, and eleven other characters, in which the reader can write the conclusion of each chapter.
    [1. Pregnancy—Fiction. 2. Literary recreations] I. Title.
PZ7.M992Sw 1986   [Fic]   86-17369
ISBN 0-915924-14-5

Printed by Philmark Lithographics, N.Y.C. Sixth Printing

Contents

A Note to the Reader

Dear Reader,

This book is different.

It's different because it can be used in two different ways: you can read the story the way you read any story, or you can help *create* the story.

Here's how you can help create the story: at the end of each chapter, you get the chance to continue the action. We give you some suggestions, but if you have another way to do it, fine, go right ahead.

Even if you don't feel like writing down your ideas, you might want to just *think* about them. Sit back, close your eyes, relax, and let your mind go. Let your imagination take off from the story.

And remember: you don't have to worry about spelling, punctuation, or grammar. This book is *not* an English test! It's a chance for you to get involved with a story about real-life people and to let your mind go exploring.

We hope you like this book—whether you just plain read it or whether you help create it—and we hope that you get something good from it.

Sincerely,
Teachers & Writers Collaborative

P.S. If this copy of *Sweet Illusions* is from the library, **don't** write in it. Use separate sheets of paper.

The Main Characters

MARIA: Maria Rojas. Bobby's girlfriend. Sixteen years old, eight months pregnant.

JENNIFER: Jennifer Bailey. White, 18-19 years old, four months pregnant with Harry Sears' baby.

HARRY: Harry Sears. Around 19, White, unemployed.

BOBBY: Bobby Ortiz. Maria's boyfriend. Seventeen years old, leader of the Sweet Illusions band.

ANGEL: Angel Ortiz, Bobby's little brother. Born with a spinal curvature.

GLORIA: Gloria Stokes. Seventeen years old, Black. Works at Piedmont Center. Gave her baby up for adoption.

SANDRA: Sandra Greene. Unmarried 16-year-old mother of a baby boy, Darryl. Gloria's friend.

VERNON: Vernon Catlett. Teenage Black kid, father of Sandra's boy.

KWAME: Kwame Turner. Father of Gloria's baby given up for adoption. Black, high school graduate, just started working construction.

ELLEN: Ellen Shaw. White, high school girl, pregnant by Jerry Ferraro.

MARILYN: Marilyn Ferraro. Jerry Ferraro's wife.

JERRY: Jerry Ferraro. Twenty-nine, fooling around with Ellen, married to Marilyn.

MRS. STOKES: mother of Gloria Stokes.

MRS. ROBINSON: Carla Robinson. Director of Piedmont Center.

SWEET ILLUSIONS

Chapter 1
Maria

I have struggled so hard for this girl, so hard. How can I write to my mother in Ponce and tell her this thing? What kind of a father will she think I am? I cannot look at Maria without a pain in my heart. When I lay down at night I can't sleep. She lived in my house and is flesh of my flesh, but I don't know the girl. I don't know my own daughter.
—Hector Rojas, the father of Maria Rojas

Mrs. Robinson, the head of the Piedmont Counseling Center, asked me to wait around until she was finished talking to the new girl and I said yes. I knew Bobby's band, The Sweet Illusions, was practicing and I wanted to hear their new song. I was hoping they didn't practice the new song first.

Actually, I wanted to meet the new girl. I wanted to see how she was handling things. It's like I wanted to see how other girls who were pregnant acted so I would know how to act myself. It's easy to see what's right or wrong with somebody else.

I remembered when I first came to Piedmont. I had

seen a brochure about it on the wall of the guidance counselor's office at school. Sometime between the time I found out that I was pregnant and just after I had decided not to kill myself I went to the office and took down the address. Actually, I went to the office twice. I had to go twice because I was waiting for a time when the guidance counselor wasn't in her office. I didn't want her to know that I was pregnant, either.

The way the place looked helped a lot. The center was in a nice brownstone with trees in front of it. The offices had casual furniture that made it look friendly, more like a home than a place for the kinds of hard decisions the girls were making in it. The first floor was all offices in the front, and an examination room in the back. Two doctors came in on Wednesdays and you could talk to them if you had a medical problem.

One of the floors above had places girls could stay if they were put out of their own homes for some reason. There was also a lounge that we could just hang out in if we wanted to. It all helped. There were times when we needed hanging out.

Mrs. Robinson had spoken to me, too, the same way she was speaking to the new girl. It was two weeks after my sixteenth birthday and I was so scared I couldn't even see straight. I hadn't told my father I was pregnant yet, either. Mrs. Robinson had helped me through that period, had shown me that I wasn't alone. So when she asked me to talk to the new girl, to help her, I was more than glad to.

"Maria, I'm glad you stayed." Mrs. Robinson came out of her office with this girl that looked so white I thought she was dead or something. "I thought you and Jennifer could have tea."

"Sure," I said. I flashed my best smile at this chick Jennifer and she looks at me like I'm going to bite her or something.

"You going to be at the meeting tomorrow?" Mrs. Robinson was slipping into her coat.

"What meeting?"

"We're going to decide about a Christmas party."

"Sure, I'll be there."

Jennifer looked about eighteen, maybe even nineteen. She sat down on the couch and looked down at her hands. I watched the door close behind Mrs. Robinson and then I sat down.

"We have lousy instant coffee and pretty good tea," I said. "And when the soda machine is working we have sodas. Right now the soda machine is working."

"I'll have the tea," Jennifer said. She was a little overweight but she had a nice face. Her eyes were a grey green and I thought she would look nice if she wore liner.

"I'm just starting my eighth month," I said. I took some tea bags out of the can and put them into the cups.

"I'm four months. . . ." Jennifer kind of mumbled to herself.

"Let me tell you something about myself," I said. "We're all different, but we're not that different. When I first came here I had the same talk with Mrs. Robinson that you had. Then I came out here and sat on that same couch. Only I went for the lousy instant coffee."

Jennifer smiled.

"The whole thing is that Mrs. Robinson doesn't want us to feel alone," I said. "You know, when you feel alone you can't think too well. I don't know how well I think anyway, but—"

"—Are you married?" she asked without looking up.

"No. Only a few of the girls that come to Piedmont are married. Some of us wear wedding rings because the guys who hang around outside the place give us a hard time. We take care of ourselves, though."

"I'm not married either," she said.

"How did you like Mrs. Robinson?" I asked, pouring the tea.

"She's nice," Jennifer said. "I don't know if I can remember everything she said."

"You don't have to," I said. "She's got booklets and things all over the place. And most of the girls who've been here a while can tell you where to find out what you want to know."

"You like this place?" she asked. She looked right at me like she was really going to see if I was telling the truth.

"Yeah, I like it," I said. "Mostly because everything is right up front. They'll give you all the information you want about everything dealing with having a kid or not having a kid. But you have to decide what's best for you, nobody pushes you into anything."

"Wish I had decided what was best for me about four months ago," Jennifer said.

"I know what you mean," I said. "But we got to live in the here and now, not four months or eight months ago. You live with your parents?"

"My mother," Jennifer said. "They're split up. She's been okay about it, really."

4

"My mother's been okay, too," I said. "She cried when I told her, and I knew she was hurt. But it was like she reached inside of herself and pulled it all together and said she was going to stick with me. You know what I mean?"

"My mother took it hard, too," Jennifer said.

"My father had a fit. He's from some other time or something. He keeps talking about being from Puerto Rico, as if that makes a difference. I think the real difference is what he thinks I should be, what's in his mind. He's got this thing, I don't know. I think if I was married he would have hired a twenty-piece band and have me marching down Fifth Avenue. All my life, ever since I can remember, he's always been talking about his grandsons, what he was going to do with them."

"What's he say now?" Jennifer twisted one hand in the other.

"Now is not so bad. Now he doesn't say anything. Now he sits in front of the window and looks down into the street. He doesn't even pull the curtains back. But when I first got pregnant—no, when I first told him. I thought he was going to have a stroke. He's got this way of thinking that a girl is either a virgin or a whore. I know he was very hurt. He wanted to kill Bobby."

"Bobby's your boyfriend?"

"Yeah, he's got a band. It's a combo, really. Bobby plays trumpet, Jose Aviles plays *timbales*, Chico plays keyboards, and a guy named Carlos plays guitar."

"Sounds nice," she said.

"It's okay," I said. "Sometimes I think Bobby likes the band more than he likes me, though. You don't use sugar in your tea? How can you drink it like that?"

"I'm just not thinking," Jennifer said. "You know, Mrs. Robinson asked me what I wanted to do about the baby. I never thought about, you know, having a choice."

"Sometimes it's easier not thinking about it," I said. "But Mrs. Robinson tries to make you come to some kind of decision. None of it's easy."

"When I first found out I was pregnant I was so . . . so messed around. I missed three periods, I had morning sickness, everything . . . before I even admitted to myself that I was pregnant. Can you believe that?"

"Can I believe it?" I looked at her. "When I started getting big I prayed it was a tumor. I figure, a tumor, at least everybody's going to say 'poor Maria.' You say you're having a baby and everybody hits the ceiling."

"When Mrs. Robinson asked me if I were going to keep the child I wanted to run out of the office but my legs didn't move," Jennifer was crying. She wiped at her face with her sleeve. I gave her some napkins. Sometimes a good cry helped.

The clock on the wall pointed at four thirty. Bobby's rehearsal started at four. Even if I had left right then I wouldn't get uptown until five thirty and the rehearsal would probably be over.

"Are you going to keep your baby?" Jennifer asked.

"Yes," I said. "I have a dream about something happening with me and Bobby. Sometimes I think it will and sometimes I don't think so. I used to always think that if you had a baby there were things you had to do. You had to get married, you had to get an apartment."

"It doesn't seem to work out that way," Jennifer said.

"Are you tight with somebody?"

"This tea is awful," she said.

"That's because you haven't tasted the coffee," I said. "You taste the coffee and you're going to love the tea."

"Does it sound stupid to say that I don't have a guy even though I'm pregnant?" Jennifer seemed more relaxed.

"I talked to a lot of girls here at Piedmont, baby," I said. "Nothing sounds stupid. You hang around here a while and you're going to hear stories you wouldn't believe, only you'll know they're true."

"There's a guy, his name is Harry. I met him once and one thing led to another and we ended up in bed. None of it made sense. It just didn't make any sense at all. I keep thinking back on it, trying to put the pieces together, but it doesn't help."

"It makes sense," I said. "You know all the biology, and all the 'how comes' and everything, so it makes sense. It just doesn't make the kind of sense that makes your life any easier."

"You want to know something else?" Jennifer had a twisted smile on her face. "I told you I only met the guy once? Well, I even forgot his name. I had to call my girlfriend later on to find out what his name was."

Jennifer and I talked for a while and I let her put her hand on my stomach when the baby kicked. When she felt it, she pulled it away real quick. She smiled, though, and I could tell she was more relaxed. She asked me was I nervous and I said yes, a little. I was nervous and I was excited. I just wished I was married to Bobby. Then I could have the rest of it, too.

"Piedmont helps," I said. "Because what you need is a place that doesn't dump on you. Mrs. Robinson never looks

7

at us or says anything to us about 'making a mistake' or anything like that. She just keeps telling us that we have to make decisions, and take control over our own lives."

"I think you're okay," Jennifer said. "I really appreciate you talking to me."

It was five thirty and I had to go home. I knew my father would leave at fifteen minutes past five. He'd be gone by the time I got home.

In a way, he was gone even when he was there. He didn't say anything to me, or even look at me. He hardly even spoke to my mother any more. It was as if she was responsible, too. She wasn't, just me.

When me and Bobby were younger it didn't matter about sex. We were supposed to be boyfriend and girlfriend and everything was cool. We used to talk about going places together. I always wanted to go to Puerto Rico and he always wanted to go to California.

When we got older and he started The Sweet Illusions band and got a van, then the girls started coming around. I knew he was fooling around with some of them. I tried to make believe it didn't bother me, but I guess it did. Sometimes I used to hear girls talking about doing it, and it was like they were talking about having a slice of pizza or something. After a while I figured I was the weird one because I wasn't having sex with Bobby.

The first time it happened was at Bobby's house. I made believe that it wasn't going to happen. He was fooling around with my clothes but I took my mind off of it. I told myself that we were just going to be kissing and hugging, the way we always did. I even asked him what he was doing when he started making love to me.

Afterwards I never went for birth control stuff because I kept telling myself that it wouldn't happen again. I told myself that, every time it happened.

"Hi, Mommy," I kissed my mother when I got home and she patted me on the shoulder the way she did sometimes.

"You want something to eat?" she asked.

"Sure," I said. "Daddy went to work?"

She nodded. I knew he had been giving her a hard time again.

She fixed me a plate of chicken and rice with a side dish of black bean soup. I loved black bean soup, but with the baby it made me have too much gas. I ate it anyway.

"What did Daddy say?"

She didn't look at me. She started putting rice on a plate for herself and then scraped it back into the pot. "He wanted to know where you were going to live when the baby came," she said.

"I'll find a place," I said. I tried to smile but I couldn't get it out, so I just went in and sat on the couch.

How could I be so different? One day I was Maria Rojas that everybody loved and the next day I was something different. How could I be so different?

I didn't hate my father. I knew how he felt. I knew that he wanted good things for me and that he was disappointed, but I wasn't the first girl in the world to get pregnant. Why couldn't he just be my father again? That's all I wanted from him.

I was sixteen and I felt like I was a hundred years old already. How could I be so different?

The TV sports news was on and I curled up on the couch and fell asleep. When Mommy came in to tell me to get up and go to bed, the dream I was having was so real. I had to tell someone.

In the dream, there was a . . . .

Pretend you are Maria. (It doesn't matter whether you are a boy or a girl.) Put yourself in her place. You have come back from the clinic, had a bite to eat, and fallen asleep. You have a lot on your mind. You have this dream. It can be a very strange dream or a very ordinary one. What happens in this dream? You decide. Write down your dream. Use the space below or your own sheet of paper. (Remember: if this is a library book, don't write in it. Use a separate sheet of paper.)

Chapter 2
Jennifer

You want me to tell you the truth. Well, the truth is I know all the biology and I knew, in my head, that it was possible. But in my heart I always thought it only happened to Black girls. I didn't think it would ever happen to Jennifer. I just didn't think it would ever happen to her. But now that it has, I'll help her as much as I can. That's all I can do.

—Kathleen Bailey, mother of Jennifer Bailey

When I first found out I was pregnant I thought a lot about killing myself. Nothing was going right in my whole life and I didn't think anything was going to, either. I didn't think about the baby much. I didn't really think about anything much. I was just numb. Maybe I wanted it to be that way.

I registered at Piedmont because a girl I know from St. Anthony's had gone there. I didn't know the girl, but she had talked about Piedmont as if it were something special. So, when I knew I was pregnant, when I finally admitted it to myself, I went down and signed up. Now I was supposed to go back for an interview to determine my needs.

"What are you doing up?" Mom asked. She looked sleepy as she came into the kitchen.

"I make a lot of noise?"

"No, but I don't sleep that much," she said. She ran her fingers through her hair. The veins on the back of her hand looked like blue snakes under her skin.

I poured myself some coffee and lifted the pot toward Mom. She nodded. I liked it when we did that. I didn't say anything and she didn't say anything. Mom liked it, too. It was something we had started doing right after Dad had left the last time. After he left she used to sit at the table and listen to the radio all the time. Sometimes she would look at the doorway, just sit there and stare at it. I used to be so afraid, because I thought she would go through it, too.

She couldn't talk to me for the next six months or so without breaking down into crying. Things were real bad. Then I started signalling her. I'd hold something up and she'd nod or shake her head no. She did the same to me, even though she knew I could talk to her. We were talking, in a way, and it helped. Later, we talked more. We got closer, too.

"You know what I was thinking?" Mom asked. "I was thinking that we should re-do the kitchen."

"You want to paint it?"

"No, have somebody come in and do a whole number. You know, cabinets, one of those new convection ovens, everything."

"It might be nice," I said.

"It really needs to be modernized," she said. "I'd like to have one of those kitchens like you see in *Good Housekeeping.*"

"Just for the change?"

"I guess so," she said. "I'd like you to move into my room, too. Your room is big enough for me, and you and the baby can have my room."

I lifted her hand from the table and kissed it. She touched my cheek and smiled.

She drank her coffee black. I can't stand black coffee. We talked about how we would re-do the kitchen, until it was nearly light outside. Then I went back to bed to lie down for fifteen minutes. Neither of us got up until it was almost nine. That's why I was late for my appointment at Piedmont.

When I got there, Mrs. Robinson was just about ready to leave. I told her I was sorry about being late, but she said she would have had to leave anyway.

"One of our old girls has an emergency," she said. "I think she's pretty depressed. She tried hurting herself once."

"Oh."

"Look, you wouldn't want to come with me, would you?"

We got the 104 bus uptown. Mrs. Robinson started talking about how the weather was changing, how cold it was getting, and things like that. I thought she would be more formal, somehow.

"Do you have anyone special?" she asked as we stepped off the bus.

"No," I said. "But I don't fool around a lot."

"I don't know why girls keep thinking that you have to have sex a lot to get pregnant," Mrs. Robinson said. "Once is quite enough if you're lucky, or unlucky, as the case might be."

"No, I know that, I just . . . ."

"Just wanted to let me know that you're not a bad girl?"

"Something like that," I said. I smiled and she smiled, too. She was a pretty woman. She would have been prettier if she hadn't been so thin.

"Piedmont isn't about being good or bad," she said. "Neither is your condition. It's about being pregnant."

We went up a small hill until we reached a wood frame house stuck in between two old brick tenements. There were some guys sitting on the front stoop. Young kids, mostly twelve or around that age, but they gave us looks as if they were older. I was glad I wasn't showing. They had one of those huge tape recorders playing a tape where the guy just gets on and talks. I didn't like them, the guys or the tapes.

"What made you decide to have sex with the fellow if he was nobody special?" Mrs. Robinson asked. Then she added, "Sometimes the answer to that question gives us a clue as to what we're doing with our lives."

"Maybe I should think about it," I said.

"Fine."

We knocked on the door and a stringy looking girl answered. She smiled at Mrs. Robinson. Her teeth were terrible.

The apartment was small but there was a warmth to it. Everything seemed smaller than it should be.

"How are you doing, Janice?" Mrs. Robinson put her hand on the girl's shoulder.

"Jimmy's doing drugs again," Janice said. "I found his works under the sink."

"Is he here?" Mrs. Robinson lowered her voice.

15

"No, he hasn't been here since last week. I don't think he's coming back this time."

"Did you call Welfare?"

"Yeah, but what I need, what I *really* need . . . ." She started to cry and her face turned ugly with it. She was pretty good looking when she wasn't crying, but when she did, it was like the pain did terrible things to her face. It filled the whole room up.

"You have any coffee?"

"Instant," she said.

Mrs. Robinson turned to me and I said that I would make it.

"Give us a few minutes, will you?"

"Sure," I said.

"Could you see if Brian is wet?" Janice asked. "There are Pampers on the cabinet."

I went into the next room and closed the door. It was another bedroom. In one corner there was a cabinet, and on the cabinet there was a box of Pampers next to one of those electrical things with two burners. I guessed that was where Janice did her cooking.

I had never been in a place like Janice's before. I had never known anyone who used hard drugs or lived in old, beat-up buildings. My parents weren't rich but we had always done fairly well, even after Dad had left. We always had doormen, a nice place to live, and enough money not to have to worry about buying things.

I heard Janice and Mrs. Robinson talking in the next room. I heard Janice's voice rising, rising, saying she just couldn't take it any more. She was crying again.

The baby was in the middle of the bed. I looked at him.

He was so cute. He was chubby with bright red hair and a double chin. He was asleep and I didn't know if I should wake him or not. I touched his diaper to see if it was wet. It was soaked.

I had never changed a diaper before. It couldn't be a big deal, I figured. I went and got a Pamper out of the box and went back to the bed.

"Hope you don't mind this," I said. "But it's my first time."

I unfastened his diaper and he woke up. He looked at me. He had blue, clear eyes that stared straight into mine. I just looked at him for a while and then he made a small noise and his lower lip quivered. He was going to cry.

"I'm a friend of your mommy's," I said quickly.

He stopped. His lip stopped quivering. He was giving me a chance. I took the old diaper off and saw that his skin was wet. I took a cloth from the dresser, hoping that it was the right one to use, and dried him with it. I felt great. I felt good. I put the new Pamper on him. It was easy. The old one I balled up and put in the garbage.

I hoped Brian would cry again. I hoped he would because then I would have picked him up. I would have held him. He didn't cry, so I laid next to him on the wide bed.

The idea of having an abortion had come to me. Mom and I had discussed it. It seemed easier than having a baby, but I knew I didn't really want to. I told Mom that I looked forward to having someone to love like that.

"Babies are great when you have someone else to love," she said. "But babies don't love back the way you need them to. They don't say nice things to you or hold you. They just need."

I told Mom that I would consider an abortion. I thought that's what she wanted. I kept holding off the decision, though, until I was too far into the pregnancy to do it safely. Then I told her that I was going to keep it. She said she was glad.

"What made you decide to sleep with the fellow if he was nobody special?" Mrs. Robinson had asked.

I thought about the question. I had already thought about having sex with Harry, why I had done it. It had something to do with me not being the Queen of England.

When I was six I wanted to be the Queen of England. I used to draw little pictures of myself riding in a carriage drawn by four white horses. Off in the background there would be Buckingham Palace, and the Prince — I never knew his name—would be waiting for me.

It was in the fourth grade that I knew I wouldn't be the Queen of anything. It wasn't the way things happened. We had a play in school and the best part, the part of the little Japanese Princess who was stolen, was between me and another girl. I had memorized every line and practised how to do it. The teacher had said we both had to do it from memory. I did it first and all the kids clapped for me. Then the other girl — I think her name was Mary— did it. She hadn't memorized the part and she giggled all the way through it. She got the part, though. The teacher said that she looked more like a princess than I did.

By the time I got to the seventh grade I was eleven and awkward. Then I wanted to be a nurse. I saw several nurses on television and it was easy for me to imagine myself as one of them. My mother said that if I were interested in medicine I should try to be a doctor, but I couldn't see myself as a doctor.

When I reached high school I just wanted to work in a large office. Maybe have an American Express card and wear smart suits. But that wasn't what it was all about. What it was all about was being pretty, being a decoration. You decorated an office, or a guy, or a station wagon full of kids.

Brian stirred. I picked him up. I didn't think Janice would mind. I held him close to me. If she came in I would say that I thought he was going to cry.

The teachers kept talking about SAT scores and colleges and careers, but the only thing that actually counted was boys. If boys liked you it meant you were okay. Even the girls would like you if the boys did. The girls wanted to be around other girls that boys liked. And the only time the boys liked you was if you were either pretty or sexy.

"Jen, you're really good looking!" That's what my friend Margie would say. "You could have the guys eating out of your hand if you wanted!"

It didn't make me feel good to be around boys. I liked boys. What I didn't like was to pretend that I was thinking of making out all the time. Margie did that. She wasn't making out with them but she pretended that she might. Even when we walked home from school and stopped off in the Egyptian store she would flirt with the guy behind the counter. Sometimes she would open the top two buttons of her blouse so he would look at her breasts. Then she would give him a dirty look and he would turn away. She would laugh afterward, but I never thought it was funny.

Even the girls kept after you, asking you how come you didn't do this or you didn't do that. It was as if they had to make sure that everybody was doing the same thing. If you weren't, then you were crap.

One little girl, a freshman, said she was going to be a nun. They all got on her and kept at it all the time. They said she was a dyke. She used to cry all the time until finally some of the girls got her in the locker room and told her that she could prove she wasn't a dyke by messing with one of the guys. She did, and some of the girls cracked on her and put her down for doing it and called her the Chlorine Queen. That was because she had sex in the storage room near the pool where they kept the chlorine. Some of the other girls made friends with her, though. It was funny. I envied the girl. She had had sex and was accepted by everybody. I was still a virgin and an outsider.

Margie and I sat at my house once and she asked me how many guys I had done it with. I lied and told her two.

"You have to be kidding!" she said. "Only two?"

I knew Margie hadn't done it with more than two guys. At least I thought she hadn't at the time. I hadn't known Margie to even have a steady boyfriend until she started going out with Frankie. Frankie had dropped out of school the year before. He works in a metal factory and he's got this van which he thinks is pretty hot stuff. He thinks he's a real stud, too.

Anyway, the day we were talking at my place my mother, who works in the Foreign Investments section of a bank, was working late, and Margie and I went to a Chinese restaurant. On the way back to my place we met Phil Estrella and his friend Steve. They wanted to know where we were going and before I knew it Marge is acting like we're out looking to have sex with somebody. Phil says we should go to his house and I don't want to but Margie says she wants to. When I said I had to go Margie starts in asking me how come I was so uptight. I was crying by the time I got home.

The next day she called me and asked me to come over to her house. She said she was sorry about the day before.

"Frankie wants to take me out," she said. "But I know what he wants. Why don't you come with us. That way nothing'll happen."

"I don't feel well," I lied.

"Jen, I *need* you," she said. "Come on, you're not the kind of girl that puts out for every guy that comes along and that's the kind of girl I need to go out with. You don't want me going out with Kathy, do you?"

"What's wrong with Kathy?"

"Nothing, except she goes in four directions," Margie said. "East, west, north, and south."

Margie kept after me until I went out with them. We drove around in Frankie's van for an hour. He was trying to get a date for me even though I didn't want him to. In the van Margie kept winking at me and I was sure it was going to be like the day before. Finally, we pulled up at this bar and Frankie went in. Then he came out and started talking to this guy outside the bar. I found out his name was Harry.

The four of us went to Margie's place. I guess it was just the time for it to happen. I had reached a point where I was looking harder for reasons not to have sex than for having sex. It just seemed that it didn't matter any more. I could have just walked out of the place again, I could have just said no, but I didn't.

Frankie and Margie were in one room, and I was in the other room with Harry.

Harry looked and talked like the kind of a guy that was going to end up being the superintendent of a building. He had dirty blond hair that he kept pushing out of his face, and he smelled like old beer. He started fooling around with my clothes, and putting his hand under my dress. I just shut him out. I was there, and I wasn't there. If the whole thing was a battle, I lost. Later, when I phoned Margie and told her I was pregnant she came right over to the house to get all the details. I tried to nonchalant it, like it wasn't a big deal.

"I think I'm going to wait until I get married before I have kids," she says to me as if I had planned to get pregnant. "As passionate as I am I'd probably have twins or something."

Sure. There was no one I could complain to. I thought about Harry and what a stranger he was to me. Somehow the fact that he was a stranger made me think I could tell him. I took a notepad and began to write him a letter. I wanted to tell him just how I was feeling.

"Dear Harry," it started, "I. . . .

Imagine that you are Jennifer. (Again, it doesn't matter whether you're a boy or a girl.) You have just started writing a letter to Harry. You hardly know him, and yet he is the father of your baby. Finish the letter. Tell him how you feel. Tell him what you think the future could hold. Use the space below or your own sheet of paper.

_____

_____

Chapter 3
Harry

So he sits there looking at me like I'm supposed to celebrate or something. What he thinks is that 'cause he gets some girl pregnant that makes him a man. It don't make him a damn thing. Before she got pregnant, he was a kid. Now that the girl is pregnant, he's still a kid. It don't make no difference.
—Joseph Sears, father of Harry Sears

"I know I can turn things around, but I don't know how much."

"You talked it over with Joe?" Mom was making potato pancakes. She was grating cheese into a bowl. I didn't like it when she put the cheese in the pancakes. Joe, he liked it.

"You gonna have that beef from yesterday?" I asked.

"No, I bought a chicken," she said. "From Raphael."

"The beef last night was good, too," I said.

"So how come you didn't talk it over with your father?"

"What's he gonna say?" I asked. "It's gonna be like the tattoo — just like the tattoo."

"How's it like a tattoo?" Mom wiped her hands on her

apron. She had big hands, as big as mine, easy. "A tattoo's a tattoo. A baby's a baby."

"Cause it's done," I said. "Just like when I told him about the tattoo. I said, 'Hey, Joe, I got a tattoo.' What did he say? He said, 'What the hell you telling me for? You already got it, you can't take it off.' The baby's like that, too. Jennifer's pregnant, that's it. You can't make her unpregnant. Not if you're a Catholic and all."

"I didn't know you had a different girl. What happened to that other girl. What's her name? Kathy?"

"Kathy, yeah. Kathy was okay. But me and Jennifer, that's different."

"You wanted her to be pregnant?" She put eggs into the potato and started mixing the pancakes by hand. Last year Joe bought her a mixer. He bought her a Sunbeam, but she never uses it.

"I wasn't thinking about it," I said. "But that don't matter now."

Now I was thinking about it and that was the difference. It'd be my first kid. I didn't even care if it was a boy or a girl. It happened all of a sudden, like a shock. The whole thing was like a shock. But it was gonna turn things around for me.

First thing I was gonna do was to go down to Santamauro and get a job. Anything that he did I can do. I can do painting. I can do plastering. I see he did a roofing job over on Kennedy Boulevard and I can do that. I can put in windows, anything. I worked with him two times before but I don't like his attitude. Sometimes he makes remarks. That's okay, now. Because now I'm going to have a kid—Jennifer's going to have a kid—I got to turn things around.

In a way I got things part of the way around already. I ain't been down to the Peacock in four days. I used to hang around there too much. I knew that. I knew that, but the way I figured I didn't have anything else to do. I wasn't gonna bust my hump for minimum wage. But now that the kid's coming I'm gonna bust my hump. I don't even care how tired I am. It don't make a difference because I won't be busting my hump for minimum wage, I'll be busting it for the kid.

Santamauro makes remarks, but he's okay. Also, he pays the White guys better than he pays the Black guys. That was what Jerry D. said. That's because the Black guys don't show up half the time. They all got grandmothers down in North Carolina and places like that and they say they're sick so they got to take a few days off. I ain't pulling nothing like that.

In a way, Jennifer's having this baby is like fate or something. The whole thing is like fate. When I first saw her I thought it wasn't going to be nothing, but it turned out like something I didn't even imagine. Like fate.

I was standing outside of the Peacock when Frankie come along in his Chevy van. He sees me and he asks me if I seen Tommy Enright. I told him I saw Tommy going somewhere with his mother. He goes into the Peacock and then he comes out with two six-packs. Meanwhile, while he was in there I'm standing on the outside sucking on a beer and scoping out his Chevy. I see he's got two chicks in the front seat.

"You seen Johnny?" he asks me.

"Johnny Tunis?"

"No, not that idiot," he says. "The other Johnny."

"Oh, Johnny Fay. Yeah, he went to the movies with Rosie."

Then Frankie starts to walk away, but he turns back and asks me what I'm doing. Me and Frankie really don't get along too tough because he hangs out with Johnny Fay's crowd, and I don't dig them too tough, or maybe they don't dig me.

"I ain't doing nothing," I said.

"Look, I got Margie in the Chevy and I think she's ready for some action," he says. Only he gets real close and says it like he don't want nobody to hear. "Her friend's staying with her this weekend and her folks are away. I want to take her home and check her out. Come on with us. I got some beer and I got a fifth of rum in the Chevy."

Margie's not too good looking. She's okay, but she ain't no princess. I figure her friend's got to be a low average. I don't care, though. Especially when Frankie says we're going to Margie's house. That means we don't have to spend no money which is good because I ain't got none. I said I'd go.

I get in the Chevy and he introduces me to Jennifer. It's dark and I can't see too good. So then we go to Margie's house and we get out and go in. I go in the hall where it's light and right away I figure I'm in the wrong ballpark because this Jennifer looks like she's real class.

Anyway we go up and we're drinking and talking and Jennifer's not saying boo. Meanwhile Margie and Frankie are like necking on the couch, kissing and everything and he's got his hand on her leg.

"Why don't you two go into my room?" Margie says.

Okay, so we go into Margie's room. Now, I figure that one of two things is gonna happen. One, is that we sit there and talk and maybe I learn to talk to a class chick like Jennifer. The other thing I figure might happen is that I get to kiss her and maybe fool around a little. No way I figure she's gonna go all the way.

"Let me make sure it's decent," Margie says. She opens the door and she's got a real nice room. Margie's real young and she's got a bedroom better than my parents' bedroom. She's even got a dimmer on the lights.

Margie takes some sweaters off the bed and then she dims the lights and closes the door. The bed is like a single bed and it's got them pillows on it so that it's a bed and it's not a bed. I sit on it and Jennifer sits next to me.

What the hell, I put my arm around her and she turns to me and she's so close that I can't say nothing because we're practically touching, so I kiss her. She starts crying.

"You okay?" I ask.

"I'm okay," she said.

She kisses me and I'm kissing her and I start moving my hands around and I know I'm gonna make out. I know I'm gonna make out.

I figure she wants to make out too because she's acting all hot and bothered and she don't stop me from doing nothing. I'm thinking about telling her I ain't got no protection. I'm this close. I even push her away for a minute to tell her and then, just before I say it, I remember I ain't got no money, either. So what I'm gonna have to do is to ask Frankie if he's got some extra protection. But if he's making out already I can't ask him to stop and look for it. And if he don't got any extra then I don't have any money to go out and buy some.

I didn't know how old she was, but I know some chicks are on the pill. I mean, if she was gonna fool around she should know what she's getting into.

"Why are you looking at me like that?" she asked.

"You know," I said.

I started taking her clothes off and she let me. That's when we went all the way.

I went all the way with Kathy twice and once with a chick I knew from the Bronx. Kathy kept talking all the time and the chick from the Bronx just kept her eyes closed and kind of held her breath. Jennifer, she cried the whole time.

Afterwards we listened to the radio for a while and then she got dressed and I got dressed and we had a beer. I told her she was really great and she asked if I really meant it and I said yes. I asked her if I was okay and she said yes, but she didn't say I was great or anything. Okay ain't bad, because I thought at the time that she was probably really experienced.

After a long time, she was just sort of laying against me with my arm around her not saying anything, when Frankie knocked on the door. He said we had to split. That was cool and I gave Jennifer a big kiss and left.

We get outside and I see that Frankie's pissed.

"What's wrong?"

"Margie's a pain," he said.

"How come?"

"She keeps acting like she wants to give it up and then she starts talking about everything under the friggin sun. You know what she said to me? She said we shouldda got a dirty movie to play on the VCR. I said it's too late to get one because Mousey's is closed. I said it ain't too late to *be* one

30

and she says let's just fool around and see if she gets in the mood."

"And she didn't get in the mood?"

"She said she would let me hold her if I wanted to do anything by myself. What the hell do I need her for if I'm gonna do it by myself."

"You do it?"

"Yeah. What did you do?"

"I got laid."

"Get out of here. She wouldn't touch you with a ten-foot pole."

That's what Frankie said. I told him I got some and he didn't even believe me. Then two days later I saw him in the Peacock and he told me that Margie told him I got some. He said I must have been a lousy lay because Jennifer even forgot my name. That's how I found out that Jennifer was pregnant, too. Margie told Frankie and then Frankie told me. Jennifer didn't even call or anything, but then I remembered she didn't have my number.

I got Jennifer's number from Margie and called her and told her that I found out about her being pregnant. I told her not to worry because I was going to take care of her. I told her that but I could tell she was still worried.

It really made me feel good, her being pregnant. It was a simple thing, a quick thing, and I hadn't even planned it. But it was like I was a man for the first time. Not just old enough, but really a man. I wanted to tell Jennifer not to worry but we hardly knew each other. I'm not much for writing things down, but I figured it'd be easier to write to Jennifer than to talk with her. I wanted to tell her about myself and the plans I was making. I spent a long time and I

wasted a lot of paper but I finally got the letter together.
The letter said, "Dear Jennifer. . . .

Pretend you are Harry. Harry doesn't know that Jennifer is also writing a letter to him. Write Harry's letter to her. Explain how you're feeling and what you're thinking. Use the space below or your own sheet of paper.

_____

_____

_____

_____

_____

_____

_____

_____

_____

_____

_____

_____

_____

_____

_____

_____

Chapter 4
Bobby

I don't know anything about it. I don't know what Bobby is doing. He's not a bad boy. I hoped he would find a nice girl and marry. This girl, I don't know. When I was young, things like this did not happen in nice families. Today, who knows what is going to happen from one day to the next. Do you know?

—Estella Ortiz, mother of Bobby Ortiz

"You really going to play at this Piedmont place?" Chico asked.

"I don't know," I said. "I might."

"Hey, man, this lawyer told me that if a girl says that you're the father of her baby you got to stay away from her. If you hang around her, then when she takes you to court she can bring people who say they seen you together and she got you."

"All that's lame," I said. "You got one of those lawyers like Jose's brother got last year. Hey, Jose, tell him about that guy, man."

Jose was taking the skins off his drums. He finished getting the last one off before he looked up. "My brother was

35

standing on the subway platform and four guys hopped over the turnstile without paying. So there were some plain-clothes police there and they arrested everybody on the platform under twenty."

"How many people were there?" Chico asked.

"About six guys and three girls," Jose said. "So they took him downtown and he's not sweating it because he didn't do nothing. Even if they say he jumped the turnstile it's no big thing. Then they start writing out tickets for everybody, but they pull my brother and a Black dude over and they say they're going to make examples of them. They're going to bust them for resisting arrest, which is a load of crap. So they're just waiting around until all the cops in the station finish their coffee break. Then a guy comes up to my brother and says he's a lawyer and he'll handle his case for twenty dollars."

"Twenty dollars?"

"Yeah, so my brother says he ain't got twenty dollars and the guy says he can send it to him later and my brother says okay." Jose held up a drum head to inspect it for cracks. "Then the guy tells my brother that he's got to cop a plea to simple assault. And when my brother says he didn't do nothing the guy says, 'Take him away,' and they handcuff my brother while the dude drinks coffee."

"Yo, man," Chico shook his head. "I hope you got this guy's name to spread around *El Barrio*?"

"I can't remember his name," Jose said. "But he was bald."

"You should have known he was no good," Chico said. "A guy who can't take care of his own head ain't gonna watch your ass!"

"I spoke to a guy when Maria told me she was pregnant," I said. "He ran the whole thing down to me."

"They can't do nothing to you if you were never married to the girl," Carlos had his coat on, ready to split. "That's what this guy said, right?"

"Right," I said. "Even if you say you're the father the only thing they'll make you do is to chip in a few bucks every two weeks. Chump change, that's all."

"Back up," Chico said. "I read where this dude had to pay like a thousand dollars a week for this kid and they weren't even sure it was his."

"That's because the dude got them things," I said.

"Golden gonads or something," Chico said.

"No, he had a thousand bucks to kick in," I said. "Suppose a judge runs that by you, what is he going to get?"

"He tells me I got to kick out a thou a week?"

"Yeah?"

"He gonna get a big smile and some empty pockets," Chico said.

"That's why they can't do nothing to you," I said. "All that big buck stuff is for them Hollywood dudes."

"You got her cold, man."

"No, I don't have her," I said. "You know she's my old lady, that's why I want The Sweet Illusions to play at this little party they're having over there."

"A Christmas party?"

"Something like that," I said.

"Did you admit the kid was yours?" Jose asked.

"No, because she made me mad," I said. I played two bars of *Eres Tu* on my horn. "I thought she was using protection, man."

37

"Oh, sweat, she told you she was using a protection and got the baby on purpose?" Jose looked up at me sideways.

"No, she told me she wasn't using no protection, but I thought . . . you know."

"Yeah, they're always running that down so they don't have to give up nothing."

"I got to split," I said.

I got my stuff together and left. Maria was getting to me. She was really bugging me. I got the crosstown bus and went on home. I had been thinking of going to the Video Shack to pick up a flick for my brother, Angel. Angel's got a bad cold and he's been hanging around the house for the entire week.

Angel's a little messed around, too. He's got a thing with his spine which isn't too cool and he's a little shorter than guys his age. The doctors say it won't get any worse, but that he won't grow.

Anyway, I went on home and forgot about the movie. It's a good thing, because he had already gone and copped.

"You eat anything?" my old lady asked.

"What you got?" I asked.

"What you got?" She looked at me with her hands on her hips. "This isn't a restaurant. You're hungry or you're not hungry."

"I'm not hungry." I went to my room.

I put on some sides and tried to cool out.

I dug Maria. She's fine and she's not the kind that goes around balling everybody. In fact, I might have been the only one who ever scored with her. All my life I've known her. When she was young, like ten, she was cute. Then she got to be real fine.

To tell the truth I didn't want to do the thing with her. I was messing with two other chicks. Both of them dug The Sweet Illusions. The horn, the van, the band—put them all together and you got a woman trap. Chicks fall in like they just got to get next to you or they're going to die. Some of the chicks that hang around the band are a little scroungy, but they still qualify as chicks.

I was thinking about marrying Maria. I figured I'd have my fling and then, when I was ready to settle down, everything would be cool with me and her. But this chick named Yvonne blew the whole thing. I made it with Yvonne and she went around telling everybody how she was my main squeeze.

"When he wants to play he knows where I keep the toy store." That's what she said. So Maria hears about it and she lays it on me real gentle like. That's her style.

"Yvonne's got a big mouth," she says.

I didn't say anything and then later when I start kissing Maria she don't stop me. Usually I grab for this and that and she stops me and I back off because I really was thinking about keeping her special. But one time she doesn't stop me and before you know it I'm making it with her. I really figured she wasn't using any protection because that's not the kind of chick she is. But we weren't doing it that much so I thought we could slide. I would have used protection myself but I didn't want to pull nothing out like she was a whore or something. Everything was cool and then she had to show pregnant. It's like my whole life went down the damn tubes.

"We got chicken and we got peas and carrots and we got rice with ground sausage and garlic," my mother says, holding a plate as she stands in the doorway. "And if that doesn't please your highness, then you can just go out to Mickey D's."

"Thanks," I said, taking the plate and pushing out a smile.

"What's wrong?"

"Nothing."

"*That* again?"

"The band's got a few problems," I lied.

"Maria called," she said.

"How could she call?" I asked. "I just saw her an hour ago?"

"I figured that's what it was," Mom said.

She left. How come everybody's the F.B.I. all of a sudden? Everybody wants to know if I'm the father, if I'm going to support the kid, if I'm going to marry Maria.

I'm friggin seventeen and they want to tie me down for the rest of my life. It's like being a butterfly. You're born, and just when you get your wings going good, they stick a pin through you.

Angel comes into the room.

"Hey, Angel, didn't I tell you to knock before you come into my room? What are you, a moron?"

"Mama says you're worried about Maria?"

"So what are you going to do, cheer me up by tap dancing on the ceiling?" I asked him. "In the first place, I'm not worried about Maria. I don't give a rat's ass about Maria. In the second place, even if I did I wouldn't need a moron to cheer me up."

"If you're not worried," he asked, sneaking up toward my comic book collection, "how come you spend so much time in your room now? You didn't used to spend so much time in your room before."

"Angel," I said, slowly. "Shut up and get out of here."

He didn't say anything. He just looked at me and left. I listened to some sides for a while. Then I went to find Angel. He was sitting with Mom on the couch. They were watching some stupid Kung Fu thing. She had her arm around him the way she does sometimes.

"Angel, I'm sorry, man," I said.

"It's okay," he said.

Mom's eyes said that it wasn't.

I went back to my room. I understood why Angel was Mom's favorite. It didn't bother me. She'd been so sad for so long because Angel wasn't strong and healthy. I remembered how she used to make up little songs to sing to him when he was little and not feeling too good.

I started thinking about my baby—holding it and singing to it. I heard a tune in my head, an old tune Mom used to sing, and I made up some new words to go with it. I made up a little lullaby. I wanted Maria to like it.

It went. . . .

Imagine that you are Bobby. You make a little bedtime song for the baby. Think of quiet things that would make a baby relaxed and sleepy. If you want, think of the tune of a soft song you know, and make up new words for it. Or make up a new melody and new words. Write Bobby's lullaby in the space below or on your own sheet of paper.

_____

_____

Chapter 5
Angel

Angel's brother got a girl pregnant? He should have made her go to the bathroom right after they did it. That way she wouldn't get pregnant. Who told me that? A guy in the eighth grade. A big guy.

—Anthony DeLea, Angel Ortiz's friend

I knew it was wrong to ask him, and I knew he was going to hit me. I had told myself three times that I wasn't going to do it. Still, I wasn't surprised when I did.

"Bobby, can I ask you a question?"

"You can't come when we play Tuesday night," he said. He had his eyes on the road. He was a good driver. "I told you that before. Even if I said yes, Mom won't go for it."

"No, something else," I said. I didn't want to look at him.

"What else?" He pulled off the street into McDonald's parking lot. "You know what you want?"

"How was it with Maria?"

"What do you mean?" The van had stopped and the lights from passing cars ran across Bobby's face.

"You know, when you do it?"

For a long time he didn't say anything. He didn't look at me, either. Then he hit me with the back of his hand.

"Creep!"

He hit me again. I could taste the blood in my mouth.

We sat in the van for a while without speaking and then he got out. It had started to rain. Once before I had pissed him off when we were in the van and he had left me alone in it for almost two hours.

I watched him go into McDonald's. I hated it when he was mad at me. I really hated it because I wanted him to like me more than anybody in the world. Sometimes I would dream that I was him, strong and good looking, instead of me, short and twisted. I used to see him walk and it made me proud. People would look at me and you could see that they felt sorry for me, but not for Bobby. You could see it in their eyes when Bobby went by, how good looking he was.

Through the windows I could see him sitting at a table. He was eating something, probably a cheeseburger. That's what he liked. He knew I wouldn't walk in there and have everybody looking at me. If I was sure he wasn't going to be mad I would walk in. But I couldn't stand for him to be mad at me in front of everybody.

Some guys passed and looked at the van. The van was tough. It had the Sweet Illusions symbol on the side. It was a drum with a woman sitting on it. Chico had painted it. The guys looked the van over. They saw me and nodded and then went on. I bet if they hadn't seen me, or had seen how small I was, they would have tried to rip the van off.

Bobby came out of McDonald's after a while. Then he stopped and walked to the far end of the parking lot and stood near the fence. He was taking a leak. I looked at myself in the mirror Bobby keeps on the dashboard. He said he keeps it there so the women could check themselves out without messing up the rearview mirror. He keeps tissues there too so they can clean themselves up if they get their lipstick smeared or anything. There was a little blood on my face. I didn't wipe it off. Maybe if he saw it he wouldn't hit me again.

When he came back to the van I was hoping he wasn't still pissed. He was.

"So how come you ask me a creepy question like that?" he said. Both of his hands were on the wheel.

"I don't know."

I was crying, but I opened my mouth a little so I wouldn't make a lot of noise.

He reached for his cigarettes and I jumped.

"I'm sorry, Bobby," I said.

"So why'd you ask a creepy question like that? I mean what do you care what it's like for me and my old lady to make it?"

"I know I'm never gonna do anything with a girl . . . ." I said. "Nothing like that. I just . . . ."

"Just what?"

"Just wondered what being with a girl was like."

"You'll be with your own women, don't ask me about mine, moron!"

"I said I'm sorry."

Bobby leaned on the steering wheel. I thought he was

really pissed. If he wanted to he could have put me right out of the van and I would have had to walk home. Mom would be upset, but I thought he might do it. I said a quick prayer to the Virgin.

"Bobby, I'm sorry, man."

"Look, Angel, when you have a girl of your own you'll know, okay?"

"It won't happen. Nobody's going to want to fool around with me."

He hit the steering wheel with the flat of his hand. "Look, Angel, I don't even know what to tell you about what it's like. Because right now I don't even know myself."

"I thought Maria was . . . you know."

"Yeah, but you want to know what it's like making love to her, right? That I don't know. Sometimes I think about it. You know, was it good, was it bad? Was it special?"

"You don't remember?"

"You want to know the truth? I didn't even think about it. I thought about making it with Maria but it was just going on right then and there. When it was over it was over. Bam! Bam! It's over! She don't feel about me that way. I know she don't."

"You love her?" I asked.

"I can't even think about it straight. If you asked me before she got pregnant, before I started thinking about it all the damn time, I'd give you one answer. Now, I don't know. It doesn't matter how you feel about a girl after she's pregnant. The only thing is what are you going to do about it."

"How come you fooled around with her if you didn't know how you felt about her?"

47

"You remember when *Abuela* died?"

"We went to Puerto Rico and all those relatives were standing around looking at us. That was weird."

"Don't think about that part. Think about the time we were lying in bed and Mom was crying and everything and then you started crying. You remember that?"

"Yeah?"

"You didn't even know *Abuela* but you knew you were supposed to feel something when she died, right?"

"Sad."

"Okay, so I make it with some girls and it doesn't mean anything. It's something to do, right?" he said. "But with Maria I feel mixed inside. I want to make it with her when I get near her, and I don't want to make it with her because she's supposed to be special to me. I don't know what the hell to feel."

"How about her having a baby?"

"I wish she wasn't going to have it," Bobby said. "I was real mean to her at first. I hoped she was going to have an abortion."

"You got to be kidding!" I said. "That's a mortal sin! She does that and she goes straight to hell!"

"She's in hell right now," Bobby said. "She told me her father don't speak to her, her mother's burning candles, everything."

"You shouldn't have messed with her, Bobby," I said.

"How do you feel about her?" he asked.

"Maria?"

"Yeah."

"She's okay, I guess," I said.

"If she was right here, right now, and she wasn't my

old lady, and she said she would give you some, would you take it?"

"You going to hit me again?"

"No," he started the van up and then stopped it. "But you see it's not as easy as you think. You don't really have to have any special feeling for a girl to want to have sex with her. You want me to get you a cheeseburger?"

"No, I'm not hungry."

He got out of the car anyway and went back into McDonald's. He was out again real soon. He brought me a cheeseburger and a Coke. He was really okay. Then we started off.

"You think you're going to marry her?" I asked.

"You're disgusting when you talk with your mouth full," he said.

"That means you're not going to marry her?"

"If I don't marry her I'm a stud," Bobby said. "I got the van and I got the band and I got the horn and I'm so slick that if a freckle fell on me it'd slide right off. But if I marry her it's different. If I marry her I'm not a stud, I'm not even a man. I can't make a living to support her. We got to go on welfare or her father supports us. The whole thing just scares me to friggin death."

"So if you're scared—"

Bobby slammed on the brakes. Two guys ran over to the van and threw soap on the windows. Then they started to clean it off. Bobby gave them fifty cents.

"So if you're scared," I said. "Just don't do nothing. You can't go wrong, right?"

"No, not right," Bobby said. "Because I got a chick that loves me, and a kid who is going to have eyes just like yours."

"No, he won't."

"Don't tell me," Bobby said. "He'll have them cow eyes like you, and Maria is going to go crazy for them just the way Mom goes crazy for you." We weren't going home, I could tell. When he was going someplace he always drove a little fast, but when he was just driving he would drive slow.

"So what are you going to do?"

"I don't know. I thought I knew this morning. This morning I got up and I said I was going over to see Maria's father. Say something cool."

"Like what?"

"Like, dig it, Mr. Rojas, I'm the dude that made it with your daughter. I dig her and I'm sending the kid to Harvard. Everything's cool."

"What did he say?"

"I didn't go. I got so scared my knees got weak."

"Her father got a gun?"

"No, man, he got the questions. Like, 'How come you were messing with my daughter if you don't know what you want to do with her?' And 'How much cash you got in the bank?'"

"I'm sorry I asked before," I said.

"Yeah, it's okay," he said. "I'm sorry I hit you, man. You get home I'll put some ice on your lip."

I think he was crying. He was driving and crying. I didn't say anything more. I figure he'd come up with the right answers.

That's the kind of guy he is. You can depend on him. I remember one day when I was really little—it was my first day at school. It was hard for me, being around all those other kids. I remember how Bobby helped me, made me feel better.

What happened was . . . .

Pretend you are Angel. You are remembering your first days in school, how it looked and how you felt there. There was something scary there. What was it? And someone or something made it less scary. In the space below or on your own sheet of paper, use your own experience to complete Angel's memory.

_____

_____

_____

_____

_____

_____

_____

_____

_____

_____

_____

_____

_____

_____

_____

Chapter 6
Gloria

I'm not going to put my baby down for nobody! Everybody who's alive wants love. Now, I'm not saying that they should just go out here and do what they want to do. I'm not saying that. But what I am saying is that just because a girl gets pregnant doesn't mean everybody has to put her down.

—Arlene Stokes, mother of Gloria Stokes

"I don't know what you mean, girl!" Kwame come up in my face like he ain't got no sense.

"Kwame, look, I'm working," I said. "I ain't got no time to be steadin' with you."

"Why you working at this raggedy place, anyway?" Kwame asked.

"It sure is raggedy," Calvin said. Calvin is Kwame's friend. He always signifying and carrying on.

"I'm working here because it's a job," I said. "Which is a lot more than you got."

"Later for all this sorry rap," Kwame said. "Yo, Calvin, wait on outside for a minute."

Calvin went outside.

I knew I had to hear some of Kwame's jive about *his* baby.

"Kwame, I don't want to hear it," I said.

"What I want to know is why you didn't come to me and ask my say before you put the baby up for adoption?" Kwame said.

"Are you the father?" I asked. I was straightening out some magazines and I put them all down on top of a file cabinet in Mrs. Robinson's office. "Why don't you tell me, Kwame? Are you the father of the baby?"

"That's what *you* say!"

"Uh-uh, baby, that's what I *said* when I asked you to come down to the hospital with me and sign up for the natural birth classes. And that's what I *said* when I asked you for money to go to the clinic. But you proved to me that you wouldn't make a bump on a father's rear end!"

"Let me ask you a question . . . ."

"Why you down here flapping your lips at me with this lame crap?" I asked him.

"Hey, watch your mouth, woman," he said. "I ain't no toy so don't be playing with me!"

"Okay, Kwame, you ain't no toy," I said. "You want me to run the whole thing down to you again? How I want the best for *my* baby, and how I know that I can't give her nothing but what's left over from a welfare check? I can't even give her the love she needs cause I'm so busy out here scuffling to make it myself that . . . ."

"Now you going into your crying act, right?"

My crying act. The boy could make me feel so bad I didn't know what to do. If I was a man I would have punched him out so quick his ass would be on the ground before the pain hit him.

I picked up the magazines and started putting them back in the rack. I knew he didn't have nothing else to say. Nothing that he hadn't ran down fifty times before. Not one good word from the boy, not one good word. Look like I been in some kind of mess all my seventeen years. I looked at him. He was seventeen, the same as me, and didn't understand nothing. Not a thing!

"Let me ask you something," he went on.

I tried to drown his voice out. Started singing a song to myself. Tried to remember a song I heard on BLS. Some old thing about Trouble in Mind. Something like that.

"You just gonna ignore me, huh?"

"I'm trying my damn best to," I said.

"You give the baby up and you don't even know who got it? Suppose somebody got it don't even like her? You never thought of that, huh? Huh?"

"You know what you got to go through to adopt a child?" I asked. "I know you don't because you don't even want your own, let alone somebody else's. You got to make out an application. You got to get references. You got to prove you can support the child. You got to prove you got enough love left over from what you needing for yourself so that you can give some to the child. You got to prove you got a decent place to stay. I ain't got all that."

"Suppose somebody White got the child?" he said.

"How long it take you to think about that?" I asked. "You stay up all night to get that in your head? Or you stay up half the night to get it in your head and the other half to fix your mouth so you can say it?"

"You wrong, girl." That's what he come up with next. "You just don't want to be bothering with the child. You don't even want to think about her."

"What else I do all day?" I turned to the fool and asked him right to his fool face. "What do you think I wake up in the morning thinking about if it ain't that child? I never had no child before, Kwame. You think I don't wish I could take care of her?"

"You need some money?"

"For what?"

"I just asked you if you needed any money," he said.

"Yeah, I need some money."

"Okay," he said. "I got me a deal cooking. Soon as it go down I'll lay some cash on you. You need anything else?"

"Kwame, I need me somebody to love me and take care of me because I ain't doing much for myself. You can see that. You should have seen the look on your face when I told you I was pregnant. You should have *seen* the look on your face."

"I got to split," he said. "I'll check you out later."

"Yeah, go on," I said.

"Hey, I just thought of something. How about Christmas? Christmas is coming up. If I bring a present round here to this place, will they see to it that the baby gets it?"

"I guess so," I said. "But you know those toy stores, the ones that sell toys on one side and clothes for children on the other?"

"Yeah?"

"Well, the family that adopted Tricia owns one of them," I said. "So don't get her toys or clothing."

57

"Yeah, okay," he said. He looked hurt. "What you want for Christmas?"

"I don't know, Kwame," I said. "Anything, I guess. You got money?"

"I ain't got nothing now," he said. "But I'll get something in time for Christmas."

I didn't know anything about the family that adopted Tricia. All I knew was that they wanted a baby bad enough to go out and look for one. They went through all the paperwork and waited and they got my baby. I didn't know anything about them but I hoped that Kwame would feel bad. I hoped that he would think about Tricia having so much that she wouldn't ever want anything from him. In a way I wanted to hurt him just the way he had hurt me. In another way I didn't. I didn't know what he could do without a good job even if we were married. Not starting out with a baby, anyway.

"Gloria!"

"Girl, don't come in here like that!" I must have jumped a foot when I heard Maria's voice. "You scared me to death!"

"What's the matter?"

"Kwame come around with his stupid talk again," I said.

"I don't know how you ever got hung up with that creep," Maria said.

"Now you tell me," I said. "Where was you when he was the prettiest thing in the Duncan Projects and talking like a chocolate Prince Charming?"

"Well, he's still pretty," Maria said. "You still think he's Prince Charming?"

"Sometimes I do," I said. I was shocked when I heard myself saying the words, but it was true. "Sometimes I see him and wish we could get together and do something good for each other. Where you coming from?"

"The supermarket. I had to pick up some stuff for my father."

"He talking to you now?"

"No," she said. "But my mother is so upset with this thing she doesn't even want to leave the house."

"Don't be sad, girl," I said. "He'll get over it."

"Were you ever really serious about Kwame?" Maria asked. "And don't laugh at me when I sit down."

She spread her legs and kind of flopped into the seat. Maria had very light skin which looked even lighter because of her dark hair and eyes.

"I was pretty serious about him for a while," I told her. "Thing was, I was caught up in that thing that said if a guy spent more than fifteen dollars on you he was supposed to get something."

"Fifteen dollars?"

"Not fifteen dollars but, you know, if he took you out a couple of times," I said. "Everything seemed so natural. You even read in the magazines about this movie star having a baby and she's not married and that one having a baby and she's not married—"

"—And talking about how they don't want to get 'tied down in a stuffy relationship.' "

"Uh-huh. And they getting their pictures in the maga-

59

zines and in the paper and people don't even want to talk to *us*!"

"I guess they can afford it," Maria said.

"Yeah, I guess so," I said. "The truth is that Kwame ain't got nothing going for him except he's pretty and sometimes he can be soft-hearted. When he ain't around his friends and having to prove how much of a man he is. You know what I mean?"

"He'd probably have to win the lottery for you to change your mind," Maria said.

"No, just get lucky and find a good job," I said. "And get his head together."

Maria stayed around Piedmont until a little after five and then she left. I was so tired I felt like just sitting for a while, but I didn't want Mama to have to start fixing supper after she got home from work. I'd go home and start it myself.

It wasn't the work at Piedmont I was tired from. I liked working at Piedmont. What made me so tired was just wondering where I was going with my life, what I was doing. I didn't have a clue.

Mrs. Robinson keeps talking to me about continuing my education after I get my General Equivalency Diploma. I don't have much faith in it but I still work at it whenever I got some time, because it makes me feel as if I'm doing something. I figure if I can just control one little piece of my life I'll be better off. I can't make nothing happen right now, but maybe I can if I get back to school.

But sometimes I just sit and wonder what Tricia is doing, what she's looking like, or what she's wearing. Then I look in the mirror and see myself and I'm glad that I gave her up. I couldn't see no way for me to go, let alone her.

I remember one time Mrs. Robinson was trying to get me out of just sitting around moping about what I was going to do. She told me about the time she felt kind of at a dead end. Some lady she worked for got her to write down two different versions of what she'd be like in ten years. Mrs. Robinson tried to get me to write down two different versions of the future me. In one version I'd stopped trying and in the other I hadn't. I didn't do it when she asked me to, but now I felt like doing it. Maybe I'd show it to her tomorrow.

First I wrote Version 1: "If I give up my hopes now, in ten years I'll be . . . .

Imagine that you are Gloria. You're writing down two things: (1) what your life will be like in ten years if you give up hoping and trying, and (2) what your life *could* be like if you get it together. Write these two different versions in the space below or on your own sheet of paper.

_____

_____

_____

_____

_____

_____

_____

_____

he time. I didn't know what she meant before I had Darryl but I sure do know now.

"If a man got a job, the city will at least try to make him pay a little something for support," she used to say. "They ain't gonna try too hard but they do try. If he ain't got no job then he don't have to do nothing. They ain't gonna make him look for no job, they won't put his butt in jail, and they sure don't care if he come around or not."

But my mama still loves the ground Vernon walk on. That's because he's always up in her face with one of his grins and his "yes, ma'am's." She thinks one day he's going to get his stuff together and then me and him supposed to be this happy couple.

He still tries to hit on me, too, but I won't have anything to do with him. All I got to do is to tell him that I need something or the baby needs something and then his nature goes away. A lot of other guys come around hitting on me, too. I know they don't come around for nothing but what they can get, but that's the way men are when you got a child. They figure if somebody else has been there, they supposed to get there, too. They know you always needing something. Sometimes you need money for milk, or for clothes, and sometimes you just need somebody to be around you.

Anyway, I got Darryl ready and took him on out to the park. I sat down on the park bench for a while, watching some girls practicing to be cheerleaders. When I see young girls like that it really hurts a lot, because I was just like them. Didn't have a care in the world. It's not that I don't love Darryl, because I do. It's just that at one time I thought I had every door in the world open in front of me. Now I

Chapter 7
Sandra

All I can say is that I'm sorry it happened. She got a burden on her now for the rest of her life. She don't know what it is. She knows what it's been since Darryl was born, but she hasn't had to live with it that long yet. You can lay down for one minute of sex, a half minute, but a child is here forever.
—Esther Greene, mother of Sandra Greene

I liked to had a fit when I started spotting instead of having my regular period. I hadn't even thought about getting pregnant again and then all of a sudden things wasn't doing like they was supposed to. The first day I didn't think nothing of it. Then I thought maybe I had some cold because when I get a cold sometimes I'm late. But when the whole week went by and nothing happened except for a few spots here and there, I panicked.

None of that old stuff they tell you about works, but I went through the whole thing. I went out and got some fresh beets and some fennel tea and took that. Then I went and got some quinine tablets and took them. I took so much

quinine I got a ringing in my ears and dizzy spells. W didn't get was my period.

"Child, what you acting so funny for?" Mama standing in front of the stove.

"I ain't acting funny," I said.

"Girl, don't be standing there sassin' me!" Mama "You using something you ain't supposed to be?"

"I ain't using nothing, Mama," I said.

That's what Mama's biggest worry was, that I w dope. The way I felt, I wished I *was* on something. Sh looking at me funny so I decided to take Darryl out.

Darryl's my son. He's three. He's small-boned cute. He got high cheek bones like his daddy. Verno daddy. You take a mistake, put some Florsheims on i and a process on its head, and you got yourself Verno come around when he get good and ready, talking a trash about his "little man."

"If you so proud about your son how come you come up with nothing for him?" I asked him.

"I'm working on something now," he said. "I got coming up. When that come through I'm gonna set trust fund for him so he can go to college."

"Yeah, uh-huh, so meanwhile why don't you se trust fund for him so he can have some milk in the mo Mister Big Time?"

"Yeah, see, that's why I can't deal with you!" he "You got too much mouth!"

That's what he's always talking about, how h "deal" with somebody or can't "deal" with them. Th tom line is that he ain't got to deal with nobody becar ain't got nothing to deal *with*. My aunt used to say th don't feel that way.

I got real bad cramps. I couldn't hardly see straight. I got Darryl and went home and it was all I could do to get to the elevator.

I went to the bathroom and saw that I had my period. I was flowing heavy, too. I was a little scared but I felt good. Lord knows I didn't want to turn up pregnant again.

The cramps lasted about an hour. Mama came in and asked me where I had been. I had taken my blouse off and she was looking at my arms.

"Why you so worried about me using dope?" I asked her. "I could have cancer or something and that wouldn't even bother you."

"I can't do nothing about no cancer," she said. "I can do something about dope."

She had this idea she could grab you and shake you and make you stop doing whatever it was you was doing. I guess she meant well. She was okay, really. When Darryl was born she helped me all the time and didn't give me a whole lot of mouth about me getting pregnant. I appreciated that.

"Where you going now?" she asked.

"Over to see Gloria," I said. "You mind watching Darryl?"

"Go on," Mama said, giving me a look.

"Why you pouting like that?" I asked. "You should see your face."

"What's wrong with my face?"

"If something good happened to you right sudden and a smile fell on your face, it wouldn't know what to do with itself."

She smiled. One of them old-fashioned big-lip smiles

that made you feel good. "Get on out of here, girl," she said.

"I'll be back for supper," I said. "And don't be kissing and hugging Darryl to death."

Gloria and I used to be best friends. We thought we were the finest things walking. She's real dark and pretty. She got turned-up eyes and a way of holding her head like she's always walking proud. She got them big legs boys like, too. We still tight but we got carried apart. When we were young we wanted to be practical nurses. Then she had her baby and I had mine. She give hers up for adoption. Everybody asked me how she could do that and I said I didn't know how somebody could give her baby away. Sometimes, though, when I wake up at night and I see Darryl sleeping on his cot and I start thinking about how I didn't have anything to give him, I can see how Gloria felt.

I got over to Piedmont, and Gloria was there answering phones. She works there part time. Long as I've known her she's always had some piece of job.

"How you doing, baby?" Gloria pushed a chair out for me to sit on.

"Okay," I said. "I need a favor, though."

"What you need?"

"I need some pills and I didn't renew my registration," I said.

"You can get them," she said. "Let me talk to Mrs. Robinson."

"I ain't in no hurry. You seen Kwame lately?"

"Yeah, I seen his butt. He come around asking about the baby."

"You still don't know who got her, right?"

"It's in the files," she said. "But I won't even look."

"Ain't you got no curiosity?"

"I think it's better that I don't know," Gloria said. "Mrs. Robinson was saying that, too."

"Where's that file?"

"Right there." She nodded toward the files. There was a set of keys in the lock at the top right-hand corner.

"You want me to take a look?"

"I don't even care," Gloria said. "As long as she's got a better home than I can give her."

"They probably don't have it in the files anyway," I said.

"They got it, in the top drawer," Gloria said. "Let me talk to Mrs. Robinson about the pills. She'll give you some now, but you got to register again."

I said okay and she went over to where Mrs. Robinson was putting papers up on the bulletin board. She turned and looked at me after Gloria told her what I needed. I smiled and she came over and asked me how I was doing. I said I was doing all right and she said I could re-register that afternoon if I wanted to. I said okay. She went into the files, found my record to see what pills I was taking, and then went to get them. Gloria went with her.

I knew where they kept the pills and the other medicine, it was all the way in the back of the building, where they had examinations on Wednesdays. I looked at the file cabinet. It looked locked. I went and tried it anyway. It was open. I pulled the drawer open and looked for Stokes, which was Gloria's last name. There were two files. One was fat, and I figured that was Gloria's counseling record. The other was skinny and I took that out and looked at it. There was a paper that said "Evaluation Sheet, Professional Staff" on top. I looked at it for a moment and then took it out.

I put the file back in and sat down real quick. A moment later Mrs. Robinson and Gloria came back with the pills. I re-registered, which was really just Mrs. Robinson asking me if I had moved, if I had had another pregnancy, stuff like that.

Me and Gloria left together. When we were outside, near the corner, I grabbed her arm.

"I got it!" I said.

"You got what?"

"The stuff about your baby." I showed her the sheet with the psychologists' recommendation that they allow a Mr. and Mrs. Harris to adopt her child.

Gloria looked at it and started crying.

"Why are you crying?" I asked.

She said she didn't know. I figured she didn't want to know who had her baby. I walked her home, but she didn't have much to say.

"I'm sorry," I said, when we reached her door.

"Let's see the paper again," she said.

I gave it to her and she looked at it. It didn't say much. Just that they found the Harris family to be emotionally fit to adopt a child. I said I was sorry again.

"That's okay," she said. "I really wanted to know who had her, anyway."

She smiled, but her eyes were filled with tears.

"Did Mrs. Robinson say you couldn't know who had the baby?" I asked.

"You can know," Gloria said. "You can even meet the parents before the adoption. They just let you know that once the adoption is legal you can't get the baby back again. I knew that."

I watched her turn and go into the apartment building she lived in. I didn't want her to leave right away. I wanted her to tell me more about how she felt. I didn't think it would be easy to put Darryl up for adoption, not after I had lived with him for two years. I wanted to know what it was like not to have a child again. In a way I felt that Gloria had given herself a second chance, and I didn't have one. That was wrong, maybe, but that's what I thought. The truth of the thing was that I was fifteen when I had Darryl. Suddenly I was a mother and it didn't make any difference how old I was. I had to take care of Darryl like I was twenty or something. I never did know much about what being sixteen was like.

I worry a lot about getting pregnant again. I don't use birth control pills all the time, even though I know I should. Sometimes I ask myself why and I think it's because I really would like to have another child. I keep thinking about how a child would love me and I would love the child. I know that's not how it works out, because a child don't love you back the way you need it to. I love Darryl but when I'm lonely it don't help much. He needs me to love him and take care of him, when I need somebody to do the same for me.

I think about getting a steady guy, too. When I meet somebody and he tells me he wants to make love to me I tell myself that he might be the guy, the steady guy. I dream a lot about getting married, that kind of thing, and getting an apartment. When the guy leaves I know I was wrong again. Sometimes being wrong is all I seem to have.

I know one thing: a lot of daydreaming ain't getting me

anywhere. I need to be more down-to-earth, more practical. I got to make a list of practical things I can start doing to change things around.

Like this:

Practical Things I Can Do
to Start Turning My Life Around

1.

2.

3.

4.

Pretend you are Sandra. You need to stop daydreaming and to do something practical to improve your situation. Make a list of these practical things. The list can be as long or as short as you like. Use the space below or a sheet of your own paper.

_____

_____

_____

_____

_____

_____

_____

_____

_____

_____

"We got to front him," I said. "Keep him away from the ball."

"I think we should split," Sky said. "I ain't got no five dollars to kick out if we lose."

"You ain't got *what*?" Billy looked at Sky.

"I thought we was gonna win," Sky said, hunching up his shoulders.

"Yo, man, I ain't worried about that White boy, 'cause he ain't gonna start nothing over here in the projects," Billy said. "But Jo-Jo gonna kick somebody's head in if we don't pay him. So we'd best get our game together."

We went back on the court and started playing again. We got the score back to the point where it was twenty-two to twenty-two and then Billy got lucky. He hit a jump shot over Jo-Jo and then, when the White boy slapped my stuff away he slapped it right to Billy who just threw it up. Jo-Jo and the White boy went up after it and it just missed their fingertips. The ball rolled around the rim and fell through. Jo-Jo was so mad he kicked the ball down to the other court.

I got my five dollars and we sat on the park bench to watch another game.

"Next time you get us involved in a trip, you better have the cash on your hip!" Billy said. He didn't even look at Sky.

"I thought Vernon had me covered," Sky said. Now that we had won he was showing his teeth. "And I figured we was going to win. Winning's my game!"

"Uh-huh," Billy shook his head. "But if you lose to Jo-Jo and you ain't got the cash, Jo-Jo gonna stuff your game up your nose."

Sky split and Billy said I shouldn't hang with him because he was gonna get me killed.

"I don't hang around him," I said.

"You his cousin, ain't you?"

"No, man, he just say that since I got his sister pregnant!"

"Doreen his sister?"

"No, Sandra," I said.

"Brown-skin Sandra, be wearing them corn rows?"

"Yeah."

"I thought you got Doreen pregnant," Billy said.

"I did, but I didn't go into no retirement," I said.

"You got to use some protection," he said. "You know you can get it free over to the hospital?"

"You go for that lame rap about not having babies and stuff, right?"

"You want to get something to drink?"

Billy got his boom box, put on a Kurtis Blow tape, and we started on over to the store to cop something cold and Billy started running it down how he didn't want no hassle with no children. I listened to him and then I figured I had to school him because it was clear the brother didn't know what was happening.

"Come on over to Sandra's with me," I said. " 'Cause I see I got to run some truth down to you."

I picked up a large bottle of Coke, the sweet kind cause that's what she likes, and a container of milk for the kid. We cut across Martin Luther King Drive and some old lady with a cane come asking Billy how come he didn't play his box softer. Billy told her to mind her business and she told Billy at least she had a business to mind, she didn't have to be hanging around in the street all day with nothing to do. Old ladies can be cold when they want to be.

When the old lady had gone on down the street, I asked Billy, "Look, man, suppose a brother run out on the street to play some ball and the man just shoot him down? What you think about that?"

"It ain't right," Billy said.

"Right, because what you got is another brother gone for nothing. Right?"

"Yeah?"

"Okay, so what if you get a baby and then don't have it. Say the girl get an abortion or something," I said. "Then what you got?"

"What you mean?"

"I mean that just another brother or sister is gone from the Nation," I said. "The man can come and shoot you down in the street or he can mess with your head and tell you that having babies is wrong. The same thing happens. The Nation gets weaker."

"You believe that?"

"Yeah, the brothers over at the Center can really run it down. You got to check them out. You take a dude like me. I'm strong, I got good health, and I can make a baby easy, right?"

"Yeah?"

"That's the kind of dude you need to be making babies. You get these middle-class faggots with their shirts and ties raising one point two little faggots and you ain't got no Nation, you got a bunch of faggots."

"Dig it, my old man couldn't put enough crumbs on the table to keep me and my two brothers going good," Billy said. "I know if a kid ain't got no father at all he got to suffer behind it. You be in the wind, but they be fighting the Hawk."

"I hear you," I said. "And you right. You got to deal with your kids. That's why when I get a piece of change I go over to Sandra or one of my other kid's mothers and lay it on them. Plus, I deal with my kids. You know, be there for them. Show him love and whatnot."

We reached Sandra's house and she asked us if we had seen Sky. I told her that we had played ball with him earlier. I didn't run nothing down about him not having the cash to back up his mouth because I ain't that kind of dude.

"Where my little man?"

"He sleeping," Sandra said. "What you doing over here?"

"Bought you some Coke and some milk for Darryl," I said.

"He can't drink no milk," Sandra said. She was looking kind of fine. "The doctor was saying that's why he was throwing up all the time."

"White doctor?"

"No, a Black doctor at the clinic."

"When he say that?"

"You remember when you was here last?" Sandra asked. "I told you he was going for a check-up?"

"You can take the milk then," I said. "How he supposed to get vitamins and stuff if he can't take no milk?"

"They give him vitamins," Sandra said. "They told me to bring him back in three months, so I'm taking him to the clinic next Wednesday and they're going to check to see if he still can't take no milk."

"I was here last week and you wasn't here," I said.

"When you come?"

"About noon."

"I was probably in school. I can't go for the G.E.D. until I'm sixteen, so I'm doing the eighth grade over.

"Who staying with the baby?"

"I take him to day-care. You want to stay with him some?" Sandra poured some Coke for Billy and some for me. "The day-care is only three dollars a day but I don't get that in my budget, I got to pay that myself."

"I ain't got the time," I said. "I got to find a hustle."

"How come he can't have milk?" Billy said.

"It don't go through his system right," Sandra said. "It don't digest. A lot of people are like that. He had a cold and I took him to the clinic and this lady I met there said she had four children and none of them could take store milk. They all had to take either goat milk or some kind of formula they give them. She was having her boy circumcised."

"Yeah, you got to have them circumcised."

"I didn't have him circumcised," Sandra said. "I asked the doctor and he said he didn't have to be."

"Yo, man, how come you didn't ask me?"

"Vernon, I don't even know where you live."

"Well, I want him circumcised," I said.

"Who been calling you King Kong?" Sandra put her hands on her hips. "Come telling me what you want?"

"What you mean?" I said. "Don't be jumping bad with me."

"I got to split," Billy said.

"Let me get on out of here before I have to knock this girl out." I almost knocked the chair over getting up.

79

"If you feel like a foreigner don't be rushin' here!"

"Yeah, right." Me and Billy split and my jaw was pretty damn tight because I didn't like no woman talking to me like that.

"She look just like Sky," Billy said when we hit the street.

"Got too much mouth on her," I said. "But you know, you still got to deal with her because it's for the Nation. If it wasn't for the Nation I wouldn't give her nothing."

"Doreen like that, too?"

"Naw, she know how to appreciate a man."

"Yeah? You think your kid gonna appreciate you?"

"What you talking about?"

"My old man is like you," he said. "He come around when he good and damn ready and I know you don't want to hear what I think about him."

"Run it if you want to, man," I said.

"Well, I think a father ought to . . . ."

Billy's father comes around only when _he_ feels like it. Billy has never liked that. He sees Vernon acting just like his father, and now he tries to convince Vernon that it's a lousy way to act. Pretend you are Billy. Write down what he says to convince Vernon. It's tough, because Vernon is hardheaded. Use the space below or your own sheet of paper.

_____

_____

_____

Chapter 9
Kwame

The movies, the television, the ads you see in the papers spend millions of dollars, telling these boys that being a man is having sex with a lot of girls. Buy this and you sexy, buy that and you sexy. People making big money selling sex. Then when the boys go out making babies, we look at them like they stupid. It ain't just them, it's the whole damn system.
—Ronald Turner, father of Kwame Turner

You ever feel like you a trick bag and whichever way you turn you got to deal with another trick? That's the way I feel. First trick was school. I didn't do that hot in school but I did enough to finish the sucker. Then when they give me the diploma I thought all kinds of cool things were going to happen. You know, like there was going to be people outside the school waiting until the graduation was over so they could give me a good job. Then I would get into all kinds of things like they have on television. I used to picture myself driving something nice, wearing some shades and talking to some cats in a bar while I was drinking some beer that was supposed to be less filling. That sounds stupid, but you ever check them dudes out in the commercial? They all smiling and sitting around and having a good time and you just *know* that's the way life is supposed to be. I knew that wasn't what I was doing, but I figured that as soon as I finished high school I would get into it.

That sounds pretty stupid now, but it must have been what I was thinking, because when I went out to look for a job and couldn't get nothing decent I was surprised. People kept asking me what I know how to do and I kept asking them how I'm supposed to know how to do something if I just got out of high school? That seemed like a cool answer to me but it didn't get me no job.

I don't know how I got to be a father, either. Whoa, wait a minute. I know about the sex part, and about birth control and that kind of thing. But I had never thought about how easy it was to get a girl pregnant. Tell the truth, I never thought much about it at all until Gloria told me she was pregnant.

Christmas was coming up soon and I got a job for a week with Bauer Construction. The guy said it could last two weeks if I showed up every day.

"I got to go over to the other job," Richie Bauer, the boss, said. "I'm leaving you, this sledge hammer, and this wall here. When I get back all I want to see is you and this hammer. You understand that?"

"Yeah." That's what I said, but I didn't know what the fool was talking about.

"Then tear down those mirrors and don't get yourself cut because I ain't got no insurance."

Then Bauer splits. Now, I'm working here with this old dude and I asked him what the guy meant. Benny, the old dude, said he meant he wanted me to take the hammer and knock the wall down.

I started hitting on that wall and nothing happened. I banged away on it and I couldn't knock it nowhere. Then Benny, he got to be at least sixty something, come over and took the hammer from me and he started hitting the wall. When he hit it the bricks begin to fly. He gave it a good start and then he gave the hammer back to me. Took me twice as long as it took Benny.

"Come on and take a break, youngblood," Benny said.

"You must do this a lot," I said. "This wall is killing my back, man."

"I done it before," Benny sat down on a table. We were taking the guts out of a restaurant so they could remodel it.

"I'm about ready to turn this job loose," I said. "If I didn't have to get some coins together before Christmas I would definitely be long gone."

"Trying to get you a little Christmas taste, huh?" Benny took a dirty handkerchief from his pocket and spit in it.

"Yeah, you know, buy something for my old lady and my moms."

"You got kids?"

"I got a kid," I said. "But my woman put her up for adoption."

"What, you ain't married?"

"No, I don't go for that marriage bit," I said. "You know, you put your head in that noose and all you get is hung."

"Yeah, you got to be tough to get married these days," Benny said. He had that dirty-ass handkerchief out again.

"You can't be no boy and take on that kind of responsibility."

"Ain't nobody no boy. You make a choice. You want to marry the chick or you don't, that's all."

"How old the kid?"

"She's two."

"What you think the kid gonna say when she find out you ain't marrying her mama?"

"Ain't none of your business, man," I said.

"Yeah, I know you," he said. He was fishing around in his pocket and I was hoping he wasn't going to snatch out that dirty handkerchief again. He snatched it out. "You one of them dudes who ain't got a pot to piss in and calling themselves slick."

"What you talking about?"

"Come on," he said, standing. "Let's see if we can take these mirrors down without breaking them."

"He said to just break the mirrors," I said.

"Yeah, we can just break them," Benny said. "Or we can take them down in one piece. We get them down in one piece he can sell them and we can ask him for some of what he gets for them."

"Suppose he don't give it to us?"

"Then we ain't got it," Benny said.

"How we gonna get them down?"

I looked at the mirrors on the walls and I couldn't figure out how they got them up there in the first place. There was a little shelf they were sitting on and that was all I could see that was holding them up.

"They got cement on the back of the mirrors," Benny said. "That's how they get them to stay flat against the wall. It looks like a piece of clay. What we got to do is to pull the mirror a little way from the wall and get a stick or something behind it to pry the cement loose. If it's dried out it won't be too hard."

"How come that dude didn't think of that?" I said.

"Oh, he thought of it," Benny said. "But he knows it probably won't work. But since he ain't here we might as well give it a try."

"If it won't work why we trying it?" I asked.

Benny turned and give me a look. He had a long face with big, sad eyes. Sucker looked like a bloodhound except his ears was small. "What kind of daddy you gonna be to your kid if you give up that easy?" he asked.

"Hey, man, getting these mirrors off the wall ain't got nothing to do with my kid," I said.

Benny give me a look and shook his head. Right away I got pissed off. I can't stand nobody looking at me and shaking their heads like I'm stupid or something. Then he tells me about how we're going to get the mirrors down. I'm supposed to hold them up while he pokes behind them with this thing that looks like a scraper which we using to get the tile down from the ceiling. If the thing falls down I'm the one that gets messed up. I told Benny he must think I'm some kind of fool.

"If you can't handle it," he said, "I can understand. I just thought you was looking for some extra change for Christmas."

He didn't say it like an insult but it sounded like an insult anyway. So I told him I could handle it if he could. So the first thing we did was to tear the molding from around the mirror. When we got that down it stayed up just the way he said it would. Then he told me to put on some gloves and hold it on the bottom while he tried to get the scraper thing behind the mirror and loosen it up.

"It's gonna be heavy," he said. "But when it gets real heavy start thinking about your kid and see how much man you really is."

I start holding the damn thing and at first it wasn't nothing. He's poking it back with the scraper and he starts getting the cement loose. The more he gets loose the heavier the damn mirror gets.

"I got one more to go, then you got the whole weight," he said.

A minute after he says that, I hear this big cracking sound and the mirror busts up. I jumped out the way just in time before the thing messes me up.

"I know you ready now!" Benny had jumped back, but he come right up on me and sticks his face up into mine. "I know you ready to quit now, ain't you!? Ain't you!?"

"No, I ain't ready to quit!" I said.

He didn't say nothing. He just went around to the next mirror and started taking off the molding from that one. I looked at the sucker like he was crazy, which I truly believe he was. That first mirror broke into a hundred pieces and any one of them could have stuck in me and it would have been worse than being stabbed.

He got the molding off the second one and yelled at me to grab it. I took the bottom and he started prying it loose. That one he got halfway through before it broke up and he looked at me like I broke the damn thing up.

"I ain't doing no more!" I said.

He grinned. He spread his lips and showed his yellow teeth and grinned like he had won something.

"You quit, right?"

"It ain't going to work, so we might as well quit," I said.

"We got two more free shots," he said.

I looked up and saw the other two mirrors. I knew we weren't going to get them down without busting them up and without me getting cut up.

"You standing on the side," I said. "You won't get cut."

"I know that," he said. "Now I want to know if you want to try to make some extra money or if you saw it's hard and figure that's a good reason for you to quit. 'Cause you got a shot if you man enough to take it."

I knew he was a fool. I just knew that. I walked around to the other mirror and stood in front of it. He didn't say nothing. He went over to it, pried the molding loose, and started after the cement. He had to get the stick up behind the mirror and push at the cement. He got three of them loose and said there was one more, but when he got that one loose it still didn't budge and he saw one more way up in the corner. He poked at it and poked at it. My arms were so damn sore from holding that big mirror up I began to shake.

"You ain't strong enough to hold it up?" he said.

"Shut up, man!"

"You don't look strong, that's for sure," he said, still poking with the scraper.

"I ain't meant to be doing this kind of work," I said.

"I know some womens stronger than your narrow ass."

"You should have got them down here to work with you."

"You ain't got no kind of strength in your arms," Benny said. "I could tell that by the way you handled that hammer."

I didn't say nothing. I was hurting bad. My arms were shaking and I knew I couldn't hang on much longer. Then he come over and grabbed the bottom with me.

"Now just let it down slow, son," he said.

"You got it loose?"

"Can you let it down if it's still stuck to the wall, dummy?"

We got that one down and went after the last one. It was harder than the first one we got down. I swear he was taking his time, too. But we got that one down and I sat right where I was on the floor.

"Come on, now," Benny said. "He paying us to get the wall down and some other stuff."

"Man, we got this mirror down for him," I said.

"We got that down for ourselves," he said, handing me the hammer.

I went after the wall again, swinging that twelve pound hammer until my arms ached and my hands, where the fingers met the palms, had blood blisters. I finally finished and we both started knocking down some plaster.

"Just so we don't be sitting down when the boss get back," Benny said.

My whole damn body is shaking I'm so tired and he standing there grinning with his stupid old self.

"What the hell you grinning for?" I asked him.

Benny looked around, then he lifted his pants leg. He pulled it high above the knee and he showed me this terrible looking sore.

"I can't do no real work," he said. "I got these people fooled."

"How you work with your leg messed up like that?" I asked him.

"I'm the same as you," he said. "I don't throw away no chances to help myself, or my family."

"Yeah," I said. "Right."

Bauer came back and he saw that we had took down the two mirrors and he asked Benny how come we didn't take them all down. Benny and him started hollering at each other and he said he wasn't going to give us nothing. Then Benny grabbed the hammer and said he might as well break them up if we wasn't going to get nothing for taking them down.

"Let me see what I can get for them," Bauer said.

He made a few phone calls and in about a half hour some guys came over with a truck and took the two mirrors away. Then Bauer told us to have our rear ends back to work in the morning at seven thirty.

"If you're one minute late I'm docking you for the whole hour!" Bauer said.

He had given Benny fifty dollars and Benny gave me twenty-five and kept twenty-five.

"He probably made a couple hundred dollars for those mirrors," I said.

"No, he didn't make much more than he give us," Benny said. "He didn't make much, but he don't pass no chance to help hisself a little."

Benny rode the subway uptown with me. By the time I reached my stop I was so tired I thought I was going to throw up. I sure didn't feel like going over and giving nothing to Gloria. But in a way I did. All the way uptown Benny was talking about what he would have done if he was my age and how I was the kind of dude that didn't let nothing stand in my way. I wondered if maybe Bauer had given him more money than I thought.

I went over to see Gloria and laid the twenty-five dollars on her and she come talking about she don't need my money. We were standing in her hallway and I threw it on the floor and walked on out, that's how mad I was.

I went home, took a shower, and went to bed. I was even too tired to eat. I wasn't in bed for more than ten minutes when my mother came in and told me that Gloria was on the phone.

I put a towel around myself and asked her what the hell she wanted.

"I forgot to thank you for the money," she said. "And I don't really need it, but I want to tell you how good it made me feel you bringing it over and everything. I need the feeling."

I told her okay and went on back to bed. My muscles were jumping and I was aching so bad I couldn't even sleep good. I was glad Gloria called, though. And I was glad she was feeling good. It was the first time in a long time I knew I was feeling the same thing she was.

I started thinking about Benny again. I thought about meeting him in about five years and him asking me about how I was doing.

If me and Gloria had hooked up I'd give him a big grin and say . . . .

Kwame begins to daydream about Gloria and himself in the future. In his daydreams they are happy together. When he runs into Benny, he tells the old dude all about it. Pretend you are Kwame. Write down his happy daydream. Use the space below or your own sheet of paper.

_____

_____

_____

_____

_____

_____

_____

_____

_____

_____

_____

_____

_____

_____

_____

_____

_____

_____

_____

_____

Chapter 10
Ellen

If I could get at the guy I would kill him. I'm not a violent man, but if I could get at this guy I would kill him. Ellen has always been special to me. I gave her everything a man could give a young girl. She'll get over this. I'll do what I can because I love her. She'll get a new wardrobe, she'll get her hair fixed, she'll get over this. She's got it inside of her, something special. She's something special.
—Edward Shaw, father of Ellen Shaw

I had told Mrs. Robinson that I wanted an abortion. They didn't do abortions at Piedmont, but they referred me to a clinic on Lakewood.

"It can be a pretty heavy experience," Mrs. Robinson had said. "I can tell you what it'll be like, and I'll go with you to the clinic if you want me to, but I can't make a decision for you."

The nurse at the clinic smiled at me from over the desk. She looked around, found a magazine, and brought it to me. She patted me on the hand and told me not to think about it. I guess she thought I was thinking about the abortion. I wasn't. I was thinking about the time I had told Jerry about being pregnant.

"What the hell are you doing here?" Jerry almost died when he saw me standing with the mop in his kitchen.

"I'm helping Marilyn," I said. "We were talking in the supermarket and she said she needed help getting the house ready for this weekend when your mother comes over."

He was speechless as I started mopping the area in front of the refrigerator. I could feel his eyes on me. I heard his wife coming and looked over the floor. I really did want it to look good.

"Hi, Jerry," Marilyn Ferraro stood in the doorway. "This is Ellen. Ellen, this is my husband, Jerry."

"How are you?" I turned to Jerry as if I didn't know him. It was just like "Dynasty" or something. I loved it but Jerry looked really scared. I reached out and shook his hand. It was cold and clammy.

"My pleasure," he mumbled. He started to take his coat off.

"Ellen and I met in the supermarket. We started talking and I told her that I had to shop in a hurry because your folks are coming over," Marilyn took off her apron and hung it on a hook behind the kitchen door. "She asked me why I didn't hire somebody to help clean and I told her it would be too expensive."

"And I told her that I could use the money no matter how much it was," I said. Jerry was seated at the kitchen table, looking from me to his wife.

"I said I'd give her twenty dollars," Marilyn twisted her fingers as she talked. "Don't be mad, okay?"

"I-I'm not mad," he said. He had regained his composure that quickly. "I just didn't expect to see a strange woman in my kitchen."

"I also told her that you'd drive her home," Marilyn said, making a face.

"Yeah, why not?" Jerry shrugged. He was just too cool. "Anything to eat?"

"I bought hamburgers," Marilyn said. "You want to wait a few minutes and I'll put them on? Or you could get Chinese."

"I'll get the Chinese," he said. He got up and started putting his coat back on. "Will the young lady be staying?"

"Sure," Marilyn said. "Teenagers are always supposed to be hungry, anyway."

Jerry went to get the Chinese food. I finished the kitchen floor and helped Marilyn put away the cleaning things. We cleaned up and I went into the bedroom with her while she changed clothes.

"I didn't think he'd be mad," Marilyn said. She pulled her sweater over her head. Her breasts were small, as Jerry had said, but she had a nice figure. "If it was *my* mother coming over he'd probably be mad."

"It's nice having a good relationship with your in-laws," I said.

"Jerry's good at that kind of thing," Marilyn took off her jeans and folded them across the back of a chair. "He always remembers birthdays, anniversaries, and holidays."

She selected a dress and started putting it on. She had a nice body and she knew it. I looked at the bed. I wondered if he made love to her the way he did to me. He had told me that she was lousy in bed, but now, now that I saw her, I didn't believe it.

Jerry came back with the Chinese food and we sat around the wide coffee table in the living room. The table

97

itself was beautiful. Edged in a deep red mahogany, the table had a delicate floral design on top and the same design in oval inlays on the legs. Marilyn used the chopsticks well. She laughed a lot, and sometimes I would catch him looking at her. They exchanged glances as if they were really in love. When we were together he gave me the same glances.

"You knew it was Marilyn, of course," he said as he pulled the car away from the curb in front of their house.

"You remember we almost ran into her in Goodman's that time," I answered.

"Yeah, yeah," he nodded his head as he recalled the time when, just before Christmas the year before, we had been shopping and almost ran into her in the department store. Afterwards, in the motel, we had laughed about it, but I never forgot her face.

I was standing on the corner waiting for the Q-10 bus the first time I saw Jerry. He stopped and asked me if I wanted a lift. I said no and he said okay and left. He was very polite and everything. Then, a week later, it was raining and he came by again when I was at the same corner.

"You don't want a lift, do you?"

He had a nice smile. I thought he could have even been a model or something. He drove me all the way home and we talked about school and things like that. Nothing big. He told me he was married.

He picked me up at the bus stop a couple of times and then one day he asked if I would really be pissed if he asked me out to dinner. I said I wouldn't mind and we met on a Saturday night. He took me to this really nice restaurant. I felt good sitting there with him. He's got eyes a little like Sylvester Stallone but he's heavier looking and he doesn't have a lot of muscles. I never liked muscles too much anyway.

We went out two more times and he kissed me just once. Then he said he couldn't see me anymore because he was falling in love with me.

"It's not right for me to sit here with you and talk about different things when I'm really thinking about making love to you," he said. "And you mean too much to me to pretend that I don't feel this way. It'd be like lying to you and I just don't want to do that."

I told him that I could understand how he felt but that it would probably really upset his wife. He said that was the problem, that he had never really understood how cold and selfish his wife was until he met me. That was the day we first went to a motel.

After that I wanted to meet her. It wasn't a thing I had to do, but that I wanted to do. It wasn't until I found out that I was pregnant that I *had* to meet her. It was on the way home, after the cleaning and after the Chinese food, that I told Jerry I was pregnant. That's when he told me just what it was I meant to him.

"You're stuff, baby," he said. "I didn't make any bones about it when we first met. You're stuff and that's all you can ever be to me. We had some good times and all but it can't get any heavier than that."

I cried. I didn't know what I thought he was going to say, but it hurt when he talked to me like that. He gave me twenty dollars when he dropped me off at my corner. I didn't go home, though. Instead I went and bought some fried chicken and Fresca, the same as we had always done, then I got a cab and took it to the same motel. I stayed there all by myself until nearly midnight. I kept thinking about stupid things, like if I was prettier than Marilyn. I kept wondering if all the time Jerry had been with me he was thinking that Marilyn was prettier. I didn't really believe it, though. I look good.

I've always looked good. Even when I was a kid, maybe three or four, my father used to tell me how cute I was. He would tell me how cute I was and when I dressed up in Mom's heels and put on lipstick he would laugh and give me quarters. That was what it was all about. Looking good. And I looked good. I looked good and I look so good now that men turn on the street when they see me. I know what they're thinking. They're thinking they wish they had a crack at me. When you look good you know it.

When you really look good you're special. You're like an athlete and you think about your body a lot. When guys looked at me like they really wanted to have sex with me it turned me on. Talk got around that I was "easy." I wasn't.

One teacher, an old hag, said I was boy crazy. That's a crock. It's just that I never got into that stuff about being a doctor or a lawyer so that people would think I was a brain or something. I wasn't made that way. Just like some girls aren't made so that they look good.

Oh, I knew what I was *supposed* to go for. I was supposed to go for education and a degree. Then I was *supposed* to go for somebody nice who liked me for my mind and stuff. I knew all that stuff. I even tried it.

This guy Mark really liked me. He was tall and not too bad looking. He was the only White guy on the basketball team and he was good. He was shy, though. He kept talking to me about English papers and what college I wanted to go to, that kind of thing. When he finally asked me out to a movie it took him half the movie just to take my hand.

Billy Ryan was just the opposite. His idea of a great relationship was him and any girl who thought the best place in the world to be was in the back seat of a car with a six-pack for a pillow. When Billy came after me I should have told him off, or at least discouraged him. But, somehow, him just wanting to make out with me turned me on. It was like walking around in front of my father all over again, having him look at me and saying how sexy I looked. You're not supposed to just want guys to get the hots for you. There are lots of things you're not supposed to do.

The doctor told me there would be a waiting period for the abortion.

"It's only fair to give yourself a chance to think it over," he said.

My mother had come to the clinic with me. She asked me if I was sure this was the way I wanted to go and I said yes.

As soon as I knew I was pregnant I started thinking about how I would look. I'd be heavy and maybe even get varicose veins or something. Who would want me then?

Mrs. Robinson called and asked me to come over to Piedmont. I said okay and went over one day. I met this Spanish girl named Maria. She would have been cute if she weren't pregnant. I told her she should make herself up and she said that her father didn't like her to wear a lot of make-up.

"Are you afraid?" I asked her.

"Not afraid, but a little nervous," she said. "How about you?"

"I think I'm going to have an abortion," I said.

She didn't say anything, just made a little face. She put

her hand on her stomach, as if me having an abortion was going to bother her baby.

We talked for a while longer and she told me who the father of her baby was. His name was Bobby and I had seen him at a dance. His band was called The Sweet Illusions, or Neat Illusions, something like that. He was good looking, but I didn't like the way he acted, as if he didn't care about anything except playing in his band. I didn't like boys like that.

Maria had looked at me as if having an abortion was wrong. I didn't think about having an abortion. I didn't think about anything except not having a baby. Having a baby would screw my whole life up. I knew that. I figured having an abortion would screw me up for a little while, but not my whole life.

I decided to get back on a diet. I thought about my white wool slacks and a pink sweater I had. I looked super tough in that outfit. I knew if Jerry passed my bus stop and saw me wearing it he'd stop and say something. Then I would look him right in the eye and say. . . .

Imagine how Ellen feels about Jerry now. She has a lot of things she could tell him. Plenty. Pretend you are Ellen, and write down what you would say to Jerry. Use the space below or your own sheet of paper.

_____

_____

_____

Chapter 11

Jerry

On a practical basis, what's done is done. Jerry has to protect himself. There's no use in blowing his marriage. I'm not saying that what he did was right. But, the way I see it, there's no real value judgment to make. The girl is pregnant. Jerry has to protect himself. In a legal way, I mean.

—Mark Leonard, a friend of Jerry Ferraro

"So what do you want to do?" I asked Mark. "You want to put five dollars on this game?"

"That why you called me to go bowling?" he asked. "So you could take my money?"

"I got to get it from you for your own protection," I said. "The way you toss down beers your liver has got to be in shock."

"I tell you Pat tried to switch me to light beer?" Mark ran a towel over his bowling ball. "She says she's tired of my pot."

"It's about time you joined the human race and got a pot," I said. "So let me ask you, you want to put five dollars on the game?"

"You give me five pins?"

"Five pins? What's with you lawyers, always looking for an edge?"

"No five pins, no five dollars," Mark says.

"Okay, but you go first."

I sat down and watched as Mark got ready to bowl. He's a funny guy. He's a lawyer and he pulls down good money but he hates to give up a dime. Not a dime.

He bowls and he leaves the seven. He's right-handed so I figure he picks up the spare easy, but he blows it.

"I think the alleys here are tilted," he said.

"They're not tilted," I said.

I bowled and left the seven, the same as Mark. He missed his to the left but I get mine for the spare. We go through five frames and he's open three times. I got eighty-seven in the fifth and he's pulling fifty-three.

"You want to stop and get a hamburger?"

"In the middle of the game?" I asked.

"The pins don't know it's the middle of the game, Jerry," he looks at me with this little crooked smile. I figure he wants to break my rhythm, but what the heck. I said okay.

At Kepper's Lanes, which is where we were, you can order hamburgers right at the lanes by this telephone hook-up. We ordered and this stringy red-haired waitress brings over two burgers that look like nothing. I noticed Mark look at his.

"What do you expect from a bowling alley?" I said.

"Something that looks like a hamburger," he said.

"Hey, Mark, let me ask you a question. You remember that girl you saw me with that time in the mall?"

"The one that could have been your daughter?"

"She wasn't that young," I said. "What she knew would make your head spin, believe me."

"What she *knew*—past tense," he said. He squeezed some mustard on his hamburger. "That mean you're not dating her anymore?"

"She was stuff," I said. "You don't date stuff. You take it out once or twice so they can play their own headgames, that's all."

"If Marilyn ever finds out about her you can kiss your head good-bye," Mark says.

"Hey, Marilyn met her."

"You've got to be kidding."

"No, I come home one day and there's Ellen in my kitchen mopping the floor!"

"Doing what?"

"I swear to God, she was mopping the floor. I nearly dropped a load in my pants. But I'm cool. I don't say anything."

"She told Marilyn you were dating her?"

"No, get this. Ellen sees Marilyn in the supermarket, see. So she wants to know what she's like. The girl's something else, I means she's really something else. So she strikes up a conversation and Marilyn's telling her how she has to get home to clean the house—"

"—And she says she'll help."

"You got it, brown eyes." The hamburger tasted like cardboard. "But while Ellen's playing her little game I'm nearly having a heart attack."

"You're out of your mind to screw around like that," Mark said. "Where'd you meet this child anyway?"

"I'm driving along the Boulevard and these girls are right out of school. So once in a while I'll ask one of them if they want a lift."

"Once in a while?"

"It keeps me young," I said. "So one day Ellen gets in. She's made up to the hilt. She's got on mascara, blusher, everything. She's sitting in the front seat and she sees me looking at her legs, see? So she turns this way and that so I can get a good look. She's real petite and she's got skin like an angel—"

"—Hardly used."

"What's that mean?"

"Nothing, go on." Mark downs his beer.

"Anyway, the whole time we're in the car she's making little goo-goo eyes, too. We both know what's going on. I'm hot after her body and she likes it."

"So you found a kid who needs attention and you go for it," Mark said.

"What's the difference if some fifteen-year-old stud with pimples on his face knocks it off?" I asked. "You tell me, what's the difference?"

"The difference is that I expect a fifteen-year-old kid to be stupid. I don't expect a twenty-nine-year-old guy to be stupid."

"Look, let me tell you something, Mark," I said. "This girl knew a lot more than her prayers when I met her, believe me."

"So you want to finish the game?"

"You don't have a shot in this game," I said. I finished off my beer. "Look, let me ask you a question first. This girl asked me for five hundred bucks. You think I should give it to her?"

"Five hundred bucks?" Mark gives me a look. "I thought you weren't seeing her?"

"I'm not," I said. "I told you she was just stuff."

"She's threatening to tell Marilyn that you were dating her?"

"Who knows what a stupid girl like this would do?" I said. "You want another beer?"

"No. Look, Jerry, do yourself a favor," Mark leaned forward. "Don't give her the money. If you start giving her money she'll keep coming back for more."

"The money's for a one-shot thing," I said.

"What is it? She needs help on the rent? The next time it'll be braces for her teeth. She got her permanent teeth yet?"

"Don't be funny, Mark," I signalled the waitress to bring one beer. "She's pregnant. She wants to have an abortion."

Mark doesn't say a word. He just sits there and looks at me. The waitress brings over two beers instead of one. I don't say anything, I just pay her for both of them.

"Are you serious?" he asked me.

"Am I serious?" I look at him. "You knew I was going to bed with her. You go to bed with a girl she's liable to get pregnant. That's how it's done, you know. Didn't your mother ever tell you anything?"

"Leave my mother out of this, will you?"

"Yeah, yeah, I didn't mean anything. You know that. You know that, right?"

"Don't you believe in protection?" Mark asked. "Rubbers don't cost five hundred bucks."

"What sense does that make? What sense does it make?

Why would I risk my marriage to have sex with a girl I can't even feel because I'm wearing something? That's one thing. The other thing is that this girl knows her way around. Why didn't *she* use protection? They don't even have to pay for it now. They've got clinics they can get free birth control pills. So you tell me, brown eyes, why she didn't use protection?"

"Is she pregnant?"

"I just told you she was."

"Then it doesn't matter what she should have done," Mark said. "Was it her idea to get the abortion?"

"Solely her idea," I said. "I don't personally believe in abortion. I can see where. . . you know, it could be the best thing for her."

"Crap!"

"I don't need your opinion, just your advice. Should I give her the money?"

"I don't know," Mark said. "If you're sure she wants the abortion, then you have to make sure she gets it in some place that's safe."

"She's going to some place called Piedmont," I told him.

"Piedmont? I know the place. It's a counseling and referral service, not a clinic. If she goes through them, at least she'll get some decent advice."

"Yeah, but if I give her the money for the abortion," I said, "that's like admitting I'm the father of the kid, right?"

"The court would probably take it like that," Mark said. "But what difference does it make when you know you *are* the father?"

"What the hell am I going to tell Marilyn if this kid shows up on the front steps with a kid? My marriage goes down the drain, right?"

"Probably, if Marilyn has any sense."

"Okay, so I'm not going to marry Ellen. So there's nothing to gain."

"Either she has the abortion, or she doesn't," Mark says. He's leaning across the little plastic table. "If she does have it, she needs good medical care and probably counseling afterwards. If she doesn't, then she needs the best medical care to have the baby and support for your child."

"Don't say my child," I said. "I don't want a child."

"You not wanting a child doesn't mean you're not having a child," he says. "Didn't your mother tell you anything?"

He reaches into his pocket and gives me five dollars. Then he says he has to leave. The whole number is this holier-than-thou attitude of his. He's always had it.

"So what should I do?" I asked him.

"Figure out what's in your conscience," he said. "Then do the opposite."

Funny. That was supposed to be funny. He left and I finished the game I started. From an eighty-seven in the fifth I end up with a one twenty-eight for the game.

Afterwards I just sat in the alley for a while trying to figure out how I let Ellen do this number on me. I just couldn't figure it. She's just a kid and she did a whole number on me. I ordered another beer and caught the first half of the Rangers game.

When I got home Marilyn was sitting in front of the TV watching the end of the game. I knew something was up. Marilyn felt about hockey the way I feel about income taxes.

"Have you eaten?" she asked without looking up from the game.

"Yeah, Mark and I had a bite."

She got up and turned off the TV. "Jerry, we have got to talk about something."

I wasn't sure what she had in mind, but it sounded important.

"Jerry," she began, "I. . . .

Jerry's wife has been waiting for him to come home. She has something important on her mind, something she needs to talk to him about. Is it about Ellen? About herself? About their marriage? About his parents? About what? You decide. Then write down what she tells him. Use the space below or your own sheet of paper.

_____

_____

_____

_____

_____

_____

_____

_____

_____

_____

Chapter 12
Mrs. Stokes

I've realized the problem for years, especially among our young Black girls. I don't have any answers. I think there might well be different answers to different situations. My husband and I feel fortunate to be able to share our love with this little child. My heart goes out to the mother, but I think we'll be good parents. We have a great deal of love to share.

— Mrs. Karen Harris, adoptive mother of Gloria Stokes' child

Gloria was acting funny all day. I asked her what was wrong and she said nothing. I know when something is wrong. I wasn't born no yesterday. Tommy come home and I asked him if he know why his sister was acting funny.

"She probably just in one of her moods," Tommy said. "You want to go on over to the court now?"

"Just why you so anxious to go over to the court and bail this boy out?" I asked. I sat right down at the table and put my elbows on it so he knew I wasn't going nowhere until I got me some answers.

"Told you he's my main man," Tommy said. "He got in a little trouble and needs to get bailed out."

"Ain't he got no family?"

"He got relatives," Tommy said. "But he ain't got no family."

"And where you get twenty-five hundred dollars to bail him out?"

"All you need is two hundred and fifty dollars cash money," Tommy said, messing around in front of the stove. "I took up a collection from the guys he hang out with."

"The paper said twenty-five hundred," I said. "And get your nose out my pots!"

"It's twenty-five hundred dollars bail." Tommy sat down. "But all you got to do is come up with two hundred and fifty cash. But if you don't show, you owe the whole twenty-five hundred."

"You sure know a lot about bailing people out," I said.

I hated to see anybody in jail. That's the honest truth. But the way things is been happening I didn't know what to do. I just heard that Earl, a boy who used to go to school with Gloria, had been killed in some kind of robbery. Now Tommy bailing somebody out of jail. I didn't know which was worse, the young girls getting pregnant or the young boys going to jail. I guessed it was six of one and half dozen of the other.

Then there's a knock on the door and it's this Puerto Rican-looking boy asking for Gloria.

"Who you?"

"Bobby Ortiz," he says. "I'm a friend of hers."

"Uh-huh. Tommy, you know this guy?"

Tommy come to the door and look him over.

"You with Sweet Illusions, right?" Tommy asked.

"Yeah."

Tommy told me that this Sweet Illusions was a band. Then he and the Puerto Rican slapped each other five and I told him he could come in and sit down while I call Gloria.

Gloria come out and see this guy and I see she's all excited.

"Where you going?" I asked her.

"For a ride."

"Since when you going out with Puerto Ricans?" I asked her.

"Ain't nothing wrong with Puerto Ricans," she said. She ain't looking me in the face a bit.

"I didn't say nothing was wrong with them," I said. "I just ain't seen this boy here before and I see you acting funny all damn day and I want to know where you are going."

"For a ride," Gloria says.

"Let her go," Tommy says. "We got to get over to the court and get Davey out."

"Davey Russell?" Bobby, the Puerto Rican boy, asks.

"Yeah, you know him?"

"I was there when the deal went down," Bobby says. "Somebody snatched a chain on the Concourse and the cops just grabbed the first brothers they got to."

"You know so much about that, tell me where you and Gloria are going."

"Maybe they got something going," Tommy says. "We got to get him out before three or he's going to have to spend the night."

"I ain't going *nowhere* to bail *nobody* out of no place until I get me some answers," I said.

"I'm going to see the baby," Gloria says.

I looked at her and I didn't say nothing. I figured from

the start she'd want to go see that baby some day. I didn't think she knew where it is. At least that's what she told me.

"Can I go along with you?"

"I want to do it by myself," she said. "Bobby's going to drive me."

"What are you going there for, Gloria?"

She turned and went into the bathroom. I looked at Bobby and he dropped his eyes. I reached over and pushed his face up so he *had* to look in my face. He jumped back like he was ready but I was ready, too. "You better tell me what's going on!" I said.

"My girl called and told me that Gloria was going to go take the baby," he said. "I don't want her to get into no trouble. I mean, I don't even know your daughter, but she's a friend of my girl and I don't want her to get into trouble. I thought maybe I would take her there and she would change her mind."

I felt so tired I couldn't stand. Gloria was a good girl. I didn't want her to get into no trouble, either. I knew she was in the bathroom crying. I knew she was, that's the kind of girl she was. She always held things inside her.

"You got enough gas to take us to the court so I can bail this boy out and then take us to where the baby is?"

"Yeah, I guess so," he said.

I told him I was going to help take the baby. He rolled his eyes up and I know he didn't want no part of it. He didn't want the part but he went along with it.

I got Gloria and we all went down to this Bobby's van. Looked like one of them things they have on television that they have sex in and the whole thing is moving up and down. I don't know how anybody have sex and make the

118

whole van move up and down.

Gloria's face is tight as a drum. We go over to the court and I tell Bobby to wait as me and Tommy go bail out this damn Davey. I still don't like it because I don't know what this Davey is about. I seen him once or twice and he look strange to me, like one of them Black hippies or those people from the islands who let their hair grow so long.

Bobby said he would wait and I told him we'd be back as soon as we could.

We had to run all over the building talking to a bunch of nasty-butt people before I could find the place to turn the money in. Then we had to take the papers over to some guards around the front of the court house and they said we had to wait until they went up and got the guy.

"You go on and wait," I told Tommy. "I'm gone on with Gloria and Bobby."

"Okay."

Naturally he said okay because he didn't care about nothing but running with his hoodlum friends. Anyway, I had some things to say to Gloria that I didn't want him to hear.

I got in the front seat and Gloria was sitting in the back. She had her head down looking something pitiful.

"They just give you the address of where the baby is?" I asked.

"No, a friend got it for me," she said.

"You the friend?" I asked Bobby.

"No, I didn't do nothing. Maria called me and told me what was going down. She asked me to drive Gloria, that's all!"

"Go on, how far is this place?"

"About thirty minutes away," he said. "Up off the Parkway."

"Get there as quickly as you can," I nudged him with my leg.

He didn't say nothing, but I figured he knew I meant for him to go as slow as he could.

We drove a few blocks while I thought about what I was going to say. Bobby asked if he could put on a tape.

"It's your van," I said.

He put on something sounded like somebody trying to knock a cat through one of them conga drums. I asked him right kindly if he wouldn't turn that off. He did, but he gave me the evilest look I ever saw.

"You know, I went and got *you* back one time," I said to Gloria.

She didn't move for a while, then she sat up and looked at me. "Got me back from where?"

"Police station."

"What you talking about?"

"You must have been eighteen months, maybe nineteen. Around there. I was living up over that barber shop. You remember we lived there?"

"Yeah?"

"I just had Tommy and things was going so bad I didn't know which way to turn. Tommy had the croup and I was staying up nights with him and the room we stayed in was so cold we couldn't get warm. How old was I? Nineteen? Yeah, that's right. Because it was just about a few weeks before Christmas.

"I was going with this guy called Pinky. I say I was going with him but I was really just calling myself going with

120

him. He would come around when he couldn't find nothing else to lay up with. One day he come around on check day and asked me if I wanted to go to a movie. I told him I didn't have no baby sitter and he said he knew this girl would baby-sit for us while we went.

"We went to the movie. I'll never forget what we saw. A picture called *Doctor Zhivago*. That was a nice picture, too. Anyway, we come back and he stopped at the corner and said he had to leave. I thought he would come on up. Pinky the kind of man if he say 'God bless you' when you sneeze, he think he supposed to get something for it.

"He said he had some important business to take care of and he would call me later. I go on up to the house, trying to figure out if I wanted to take you and Tommy down to the Chinese place and get me some fried rice. I knock on the door and you open it up. Your nose was all snotty. Tommy he done mess all over himself, and this girl is long gone. The first thing I did was to look where I kept my money. My whole check was gone. And you know what was the hurting thing?"

"Your check being gone," Bobby said.

"Uh-uh, that's not what hurt," I said. "That made me mad but it didn't hurt. What hurt me was that I knew I didn't have a damn thing else to look forward to in my life. There wasn't no jobs I could get was going to pay as much as the welfare because I didn't have no school behind me. I lay across that bed and cried and asked Jesus if He couldn't have thought of something better for me than that.

"That's when I decided that I couldn't do nothing for you. I put your little red coat on and took you over near Goodman's. The way you looked at me I thought you knew what I was going to do. I took you right in front of the store and then I told you to wait there for me for a minute. I went in the department store and out the side door.

"Then I went home and cried all night. Lord, I just felt so miserable. I just felt so miserable. My mind just kept picturing you standing on the corner crying, and I thought that maybe somebody bad got you or something.

"About one o'clock in the morning I couldn't stand it no longer. I got Tommy and went over to Goodman's and waited until I saw a patrol car. I told the policeman I had lost a little baby and he didn't say a word to me. He didn't say a word to me, not a word. He opened the back door and told me to get in. Then he just went on talking to his partner about going bowling, or something. He took me over to the precinct and they had you in the back waiting for somebody from the Welfare department to pick you up. Girl, when you seen me. . . ."

"Don't cry, Mama," Gloria put her arms around my shoulder.

". . .When you seen me your little eyes lit up and you come running across the room. And I was standing there in my old coat without even carfare to get us back home. I didn't have a thing for you girl."

"Don't cry, Mama."

I was crying but I pulled myself together. Bobby gave me a tissue from a box he had on his dashboard and I blew my nose.

"The desk sergeant got my name and I tried to tell him the whole story, about Pinky, and the girl stealing my money, and everything. He said he didn't really want to hear my story. He said, 'Lady, if I could do a damn thing about it maybe I would listen. But I can't so there's no use wasting my time.'"

"That was cold," Bobby said. "Cops are some cold-ass suckers."

"Every word he said was true," I said. "He couldn't change a thing and I ain't changed a thing. All them dreams I had when I was coming up was just like the name on this van, they was illusions. I guess they was sweet when I was reaching for them, too. I ain't saying it got to be that way for everybody or for all the time. All I'm saying is that sometimes it be's that way, and yours ain't the only heart's going to break if you don't let yourself see it."

We drove around some more and then Bobby pulled up across from where Gloria's baby was. It was an apartment house. It looked nice. It wasn't no palace, but it was nice. We sat in the van for a while and looked out across the street. Some people were leaving the building. They had a baby, but it wasn't Gloria's, it was too young.

Some children were playing on the sidewalk.

"Honey, you can't do nothing for her. You love her, and you need her because you're like I was. You ain't got nobody else to love and need, not like you can love and need a man or a baby. The people who got it, they got good jobs and they going to love your baby as much as you do, maybe even more. That's a hard thing to say, but it's true. Because sooner or later you're going to find out that your baby can't love you back in the way you need it to. And there are going to be times when you just can't help resenting her. Don't put that hurt on your child, Gloria. Give your baby the chance you didn't have, honey."

Gloria put her arm around me, and I put mine around

her. Bobby patted Gloria on the shoulder and she put her arm around him and we just all sat there and held each other for a while.

"It's a nice block," Gloria said.

"It is," I said.

"Guess we might as well go on home, now," she said.

Bobby didn't say nothing, he just started the van, and we went on.

When we got home Gloria went straight to her room and went to bed. I could hear her crying, and I knew she was hurting something terrible. I wanted to go in to her, to comfort her, but I didn't want to answer the question I thought she might want to ask. If she asks it, if she asks me if I had ever been sorry I had gone back for her, I would say. . . .

This one is tough. Pretend you are Mrs. Stokes. You are only about 35 years old but already a grandmother. You have just told Gloria something that you've kept hidden from her all these years: you once abandoned her. If Gloria now asked you if you've ever been sorry for going back to get her, what do you say? Think about it and write down Mrs. Stokes' answer. Use the space below or your own sheet of paper.

_____

_____

_____

_____

Chapter 13
Mrs. Robinson

Mom really enjoys working with the girls and I think she respects them. Usually the girl isn't thinking or she's reached a point in her life where it really doesn't make that much difference. At least it looks to her like it doesn't make that much difference if she has a baby or not. Would I work at Piedmont? I might if it paid more.

—Doris Simons, daughter of Carla Robinson

"I think this is going to be a nice party," Maria announced. She had cut out and glued the paper creche and put it under the small tree. Her baby, Alex, lay in his folding bassinet.

"I hope so," I said.

"How can Christmas be bad?" Jennifer had come to help with the last-minute decorations.

"Sometimes these parties are very sad," I said. "The people here all have problems. No matter if a pregnancy is a joy or a disaster for the mother, it's always a problem. How are you feeling, Maria?"

"Pretty good," she said. "I had the stitches taken out Monday. I hated that."

Jennifer was hanging a wreath and stopped to turn to Maria. "It hurt?"

"No, but I thought my regular doctor was going to do it," Maria said. "He comes in with this young doctor and he examines me and the young doctor is there. Then he tells the young doctor to take the stitches out. It's embarrassing."

"It's a clinic," I said.

"I'm surprised you can bring him out so soon," Jennifer said.

"You're excited about your baby, aren't you?" Maria smiled.

"A little," Jennifer said. She sat down and folded her hands in her lap. "I'm excited, and I'm scared. My mother is excited, too. It's as if we're going through it together. It helps a lot."

"Have you spoken to your father, Maria?" I asked.

"No. He hasn't spoken a word to me. I called the other day. . . ." Her voice broke. "He answered the phone. I said hello and there was no answer. Then he hung the phone up. He won't even speak to me on the phone. He hasn't seen the baby or anything. Mommy told me this morning that he asked what I was doing with myself. She told him about the party here today and he just grunted, the way he does when he's mad."

I put my arms around Maria. I had done the same to so many girls over the years. They were all so hurt when the people they loved most turned against them when they became pregnant. It was as if they had done something so terrible that all the world should shun them. They hadn't done anything terrible. What they had done was to complicate their lives and the lives of the children they had brought into

128

the world. That and nothing more.

"I bet you're having fun fixing up your new place," Jennifer said, taking a tissue and wiping Maria's face with it. "You going to invite me over for tea?"

"It's a terrible place," Maria said. "The lady from the Welfare came and saw it yesterday. 'Oh, what a lovely little place,' she said. I bet *she* wouldn't live in it."

"It wouldn't help very much to say that it was a bad looking place," I said. "Is it warm?"

"It's warm, and they've got two locks on the door, so I'll be all right. My mother hasn't seen it. I have to fix it up before she comes over."

"I've got some things," I said. "Some curtains and a nice bedspread. I'll bring them over. Maybe Jennifer can come and we can all have tea."

"Mrs. Robinson?" Maria looked at me. Alex turned in his sleep and she jumped a little.

"Oh, you're such a nervous little mother!" Jennifer gave Maria a friendly jab.

"He's so tiny!" Maria said. "I think if I squeezed him hard I could break him."

"You can't break them that easily," I said. "Were you going to ask me something?"

"Yeah. How did you get into this business? I mean, you're just perfect for it."

"Same way that you did," I said. "I was a teenage mother, unmarried, and I went to a place more or less like this one. I got lucky and was able to go back to school for a degree. I started working in Piedmont in '74 and I've been here ever since."

"You have a son?"

"Daughter. She's eighteen and, if God or the saints give her a few answers on her math finals, she might even graduate high school this year."

The phone rang. I went to answer it in the office. Through the glass I could see Maria and Jennifer fussing with Maria's baby. They were like two children playing dolls.

It was Ellen. I listened to her and told her that I understood.

Ellen said, "I had the abortion because I just, you know, couldn't go through with the baby and everything. I got the money from my grandmother. I asked the guy for the money but he kept talking about how did he know it was his baby. I *told* him it was his baby."

"Sometimes. . . ." Sometimes the job was hard. "Sometimes guys just can't bring themselves to do the right things."

"Anyway, I don't feel so good, so I won't be coming to the party."

"Are you bleeding or anything?"

"No, I feel okay that way," Ellen said. "I'm just down, you know."

"Yes, I know. Look, will you come around during the holidays? We can just talk."

"Would you mind?"

"Not at all."

"Okay, maybe I will. Tell the girls hello for me, okay?"

"Sure."

By the time I was off the phone four other girls and two guys had shown up. I told them that Ellen couldn't make it, but that she seemed okay.

Bobby showed up with a tape player and some tapes.

There was a strain between him and Maria. All of a sudden there was a baby in their lives, a baby that belonged to both of them, and they didn't know how to act.

He looked down at the baby, at his child, and I saw him searching for words. Maria picked the baby up casually and walked away with him to talk to Jennifer. She wasn't going to make it that easy for Bobby.

"Hey, you want some Christmas music or some regular music?" Bobby asked.

"Christmas music," answered Gloria as she came in. Her mother came in with her.

"How you doing?" Mrs. Stokes smiled at me broadly.

"Good," I said. "I'm glad you could make it."

"I was at the party here last year, too, remember?" she said.

Jennifer served the punch. Some women from the family planning clinic came in with toys that had been sent over from the Fire Department. Gloria tried to get Bill, from the maintenance staff, to dance.

"Mrs. Robinson, tell this dude he has to dance with us," Gloria said.

"It's a rule, Bill," I kidded him. "You either have to dance or change the baby if he gets wet."

"I'll dance," Bill said.

How they managed to dance to "O Tannenbaum" I didn't know, but they were dancing. Everyone was laughing. Maria let people hold her baby, but she kept a watchful eye on him. So many of the young girls had to be taught to take care of their children. There were a lot of things that Maria had to learn, but I could see she would learn them more easily than some.

Two teenage boys came in. Sometimes boys wandered in from off the street just to see what we were doing at Piedmont. These two seemed to know Gloria.

"That's Gloria's baby's father," Mrs. Stokes said. "He's a nice boy but she don't want to marry him."

"Does he want to marry her?"

"He halfway do," Mrs. Stokes said. "He's talking about getting into some kind of training program, but I don't think he see nothing clear for himself."

"They get some heavy responsibilities for young people without a lot of experience," I said.

"What any of them know?" Bobby had turned the tape player up and Mrs. Stokes had to raise her voice to be heard over it. "They just babies having babies."

"I guess you're right," I said.

"Kwame!" Mrs. Stokes called him over. I recognized him when he came closer. I had seen him around Piedmont before.

"How you doing?" He had his hat on the side of his head.

"Kwame, this is Mrs. Robinson," Mrs. Stokes introduced us and I nodded.

"This is a nice little party," he said, a toothpick dangled from the corner of his mouth. "You people do a good job. What you do, get money from the government to run this place?"

"Part of our funding is from the government," I said.

"Yeah, well you keep up the good work," he said. "I got to check out the punch."

"Ain't he something?" Mrs. Stokes said.

"You like him?"

"I guess he ain't no different than the rest," she answered.

"I think Gloria can be," I said.

Sandra showed up. I had asked her to, after I found out what had happened with Gloria's records. I told Sandra what I thought about what she had done. She said that she thought she had done the right thing, but realized later that she hadn't. I accepted it, but I really didn't believe it.

I didn't believe it because so many of the young girls seemed not to be sympathetic to each other. So many of them would make trouble for each other. It was almost as if they hated the position they found themselves in and hated anyone else who got into it. But I had asked her to come to the party. I didn't want her to stay away and not get the kinds of information and materials that she needed. It wouldn't help if she got pregnant again.

The party had settled down somewhat. The girls were mostly sitting around talking and the boys, for some strange reason, were sitting by themselves around the tape recorder. It was as if they really weren't connected. Then the door opened and a big, older man appeared in it. He seemed to fill the frame with his bulk.

He looked upset and I thought at first it might have been one of the people who seemed to hate clinics such as Piedmont, who believed that we were somehow trying to do something evil in it. Then I saw Jennifer touch Maria's arm.

Maria looked at the man, then stood quickly and went to where Sandra was holding little Alex. She took her baby from Sandra and went to the bassinet, where she laid him down gently and stood next to him.

I got up instinctively. We had had trouble at Piedmont

133

before. The man walked toward the bassinet and the baby, and I went quickly across the room.

"Hello," I extended my hand toward him. He looked at me, and at my hand, and then toward the baby. There were small drops of sweat on his forehead. "Is there anything I can do for you?"

He moved toward the bassinet and I started to stop him, but Maria took my arm. "He's my father," she said.

There were tears in his eyes as he looked down at the baby. He looked at the baby, breathing heavily, his wide, rounded shoulders moving with each breath. I was nervous. I thought about calling the police.

He sighed heavily and looked toward Maria. Her eyes were wide. There was a movement to my right and Bobby came over and picked up the baby. He stood next to Maria. She put her hand on his arm and held on for dear life.

"A boy," the man said, finally.

Maria started to speak, couldn't, and just nodded her head.

The man looked at Bobby. Bobby straightened up. He looked so young.

"You finish here, you come home," the man said to Maria.

Maria went to him and he put his arms around her. She was crying against his chest and he patted her gently on the shoulder. Then he looked over her shoulder at Bobby. He nodded, turned, and then left.

The boy who came with Bobby put on a tape of "O Holy Night," and said that it would sound better with some congas behind it.

When the party was over and everyone had left I sat

alone in my office for a while. I thought about a girl who had been at Piedmont when I first became director. Her parents had put her out of their home, and she was staying at the center. She came to me one afternoon shortly before Christmas. She was crying.

"It isn't fair," she said. "I'm not a bad person, why am I going through this?"

I didn't know what to say to her. I just held her close for a very long time.

The government has asked Mrs. Robinson to write a report telling why the Piedmont Counseling Center should receive funds. Pretend you are Mrs. Robinson. Write down why Piedmont deserves funding. Use the space below or your own sheet of paper.

_____

_____

_____

_____

_____

_____

_____

_____

_____

_____

Chapter 14
Jennifer --
Seven Years Later

I wasn't easy about going back to Piedmont. There were a lot of memories associated with the quiet brownstone building, only some of them pleasant. I had read in the paper that they were expanding their services to include a day-care center for girls finishing high school. But the thing that attracted me most was the name of the director, Gloria Stokes Turner. My nervousness disappeared when Gloria came out of her office with a tall young girl, no more than fifteen, and very much pregnant. When she had said good-bye to the girl I tiptoed over and said, "Hey, lady."

"Jennifer?" Gloria put on a pair of rimless glasses and took a good look at me. "Jennifer!"

We hugged and both started talking at once. I wanted to cry I was so happy to see her. It had been a long time.

"How long have you been the director here?" I asked.

"A little over a year now," Gloria said, smoothing her skirt as she sat down. "You look great, tell me about yourself."

"What do you want to know?" I asked.

"First, the girl stuff," Gloria said. "How's your son, how's your life. You married? What are you doing?"

"I'm not married," I said. "And right now there's nobody who's getting that close. Paul, that's my son, is fine. He's going into the second grade this year. Let's see, I'm working with an advertising firm as an account executive, and still living in the same place with my mother. I guess I've kind of let my career be the center of my life."

"You look good. Are you jogging or something?"

"I go to a health club when I can find the time," I said. "When I came in here today I saw some of the girls sitting around, I thought about us seven years ago."

"Has it been *that* long?"

"Seven years and four months since I first came to Piedmont," I said. "Now, tell me about yourself."

"Well, Mrs. Robinson convinced me to finish high school and then I started college at night. It was more something to do than anything else, at first. Then I saw that with a lot of work I could make it in college, so I stuck to it."

"You were always pretty smart," I said.

"I don't know about that," Gloria said. "I was as scared of going into the college as I was of coming here for the first time."

"Then what?"

"Halfway through my second year at night I met up with Kwame again. He was working as a guard and generally being Kwame. But he was studying for the Post Office. I helped him get ready for the test and he passed it. We started seeing each other and before I knew it, I found myself walking down the aisle with the guy. He was working in the post office by then and I went to school full time and worked at Piedmont part time. When I finished there was an opening here for director."

"Mrs. Robinson left?"

"To work in Chicago," Gloria said. "She's heading a big education project out there."

"Any more children?"

"Not yet, but we're thinking about it now," Gloria said. "We struggled so the first years that we decided to wait. I would have liked to have had Tricia, but I think the only reason Kwame and I made it was because we didn't have the pressure of a child. Now my mother's talking about how she wants a grandchild and I think Kwame's ready."

"My mother helps a lot with Paul," I said. "But it's still hard sometimes. Have you seen anyone else?"

"You remember Bobby and Maria?"

"Yeah."

"They've got five children, she's about thirty pounds too heavy, and he's got a pot belly and spends most of his time in front of the television set."

"Bobby? That doesn't sound like him!"

"Isn't it the truth? He was always so on the move!" Gloria moved her shoulders to a remembered beat. "But how could you tell what any of us were going to be? We didn't even know who we were back then. I guess you haven't seen — I can't remember his name. . . ."

"Harry," I said. "I did see him. I looked him up, thinking that maybe I owed it to Paul to introduce him to his father. Somehow Harry managed to stay at the same place he was in seven years ago. He drinks pretty heavily, I think. He had his own problems. He wasn't interested in either me or his son. I talked to him on a street corner. We were strangers. I think he was as uncomfortable as I was."

"You remember Sandra?"

"Not too well," I said. "Was she blonde?"

"No, Black," Gloria said. "She's had two more children. She has three in all. She's on welfare and living in the Currie Woods projects. She seems happy enough, but I know she wanted more out of life than she's getting."

"How about that cute little girl, the redhead."

"Ellen," Gloria's voice changed slightly. "She's been married about three times. Sometimes, when she's depressed, she calls and says she wants to drop by to talk and we make an appointment, but she never comes."

"Is she sorry about the abortion?"

"No, I don't think so. Just confused about her life," Gloria said. "I don't think all of the questions have answers, Jennifer. I used to think they did, and that I just didn't know them, but now I'm not sure."

"I'm glad to hear that you and Kwame are doing well," I said.

"Sometimes we are, and sometimes we're not," Gloria said. "But he seems to be willing to work at it all the time. He doesn't give it up, so I think we're going to make it."

"I've got to run. My mother's keeping Paul. Maybe we can get together for dinner sometime?"

141

"I'd like that," she said. "Maybe I can get you to do some volunteer counselling at the center?"

"We'll see," I said. "I might like that."

On the way home I thought about Gloria, about how she had changed. I knew it had been hard for her to give her daughter up for adoption, but it had given her — and her daughter — another chance.

I thought about some of the others, Maria, Ellen, and Sandra. I thought about the guys, too. For some of them, kids seven years ago, things had worked out. For some, it hadn't. I didn't know if our problems had started with our pregnancies, or long before. I knew having kids when we were that young hadn't helped any of us.

I didn't know what the answers were, either. I didn't know if I would have been better off not keeping Paul, or what. I knew it was hard raising him without a father. I thought it would have been just as hard, maybe harder, trying to raise him with Harry.

The subway ride home was murder and I had to get off and walk over to the delicatessen to get something for Paul to eat. Mom had probably fed him, but then again, maybe she hadn't. In the deli I ordered two corned beef sandwiches and wrote down Gloria's number in my appointment book.